The Boy Who Dreamed

Kent Raddatz

Twelve-year-old Jacob Tannin is being bullied by Willard and doesn't know what to do about it. He pretends to be invisible in the hopes that Willard will pick on someone else. It doesn't work. And sometimes, while he's being picked on, something sarcastic pops out of his mouth—which never goes over well.

But Jacob's also a dreamer. And when his dreams take him to another world called Chimeran, things begin to change. In Chimeran, he's attacked by Haggeldies, a new set of bullies. But he also makes friends who try to teach him how to stand up for himself.

As he goes back and forth between these two worlds, he's forced to see others in a new way. And he's encouraged to learn the power that comes from what he believes about himself.

Will Jacob ever stop being afraid? What will give him the courage to speak up for himself? And how will he learn what he's worth when bullies in both worlds say he's nothing?

Print ISBN: 979-8638-8225-07

Independently published by Kent Raddatz

Acknowledgments

*"Maybe one day we will find
the place where our dreams
and reality collide."*

With thanks to my wife who supports me in everything I do and is the place where my dreams and reality meet. With thanks to my parents who always encouraged me to be who I am and to do what I want. With thanks to my sisters who helped me in the process of writing. With thanks to my daughter-in-law, Amy, for creating my web page and the cover of this book. With thanks to Lisa Lickel, who encouraged me in my writing and taught me about the process.

This book is dedicated to my grandchildren:
Misty, Alli, Angel, Isaac, Kati, Lyle, and Ava who
are perfect in every way.

Contents

Author's Comments

We live in an age of bullying where those who want their way feel astonishingly comfortable saying or doing whatever they want—while assuming they won't be held accountable. Every child needs to know this is unacceptable behavior for anyone, no matter their station in life.

All the bullies I've encountered were cowards underneath. They used their size and aggressiveness to cover up their weaknesses. I suppose they thought this would make them look more impressive or important than they were (or than they thought they were). It's too bad they didn't learn to respect others so they could then feel good about themselves.

Yet, this book is not about the bullies. It's about those who are being called names, "put in their place," pushed aside, or knocked down. These are the ones who need encouragement and support. My hope is to provide some of that through this story.

Chapter One – Running Away

Like a firefighter getting ready to knock down a wave of flames, Jacob planted his feet, adjusted his grip on the garden hose and looked up at his target: a giant hornet's nest under construction in the highest peak of the roof. He pulled his goggles down and then sprayed and sprayed till those nasty flying bugs and everything around them were soaked.

When they came after him for revenge, Jacob dropped the hose, ripped the goggles from his face and took off toward the ditch, fifty yards away. As he raced past the white birch in the center of the yard, he gave one of its branches a high five for luck. Halfway to the ditch, the hornets gave up the chase. *"Too slow, too slow,"* he repeated as he shuffled his feet and waved his arms to celebrate.

He was proud of the fact that in all the times he'd drowned their nests, he'd never once been stung. That's because his greatest talent, as a twelve-year-old boy, was running away. But, of course, the reason he was so good at it had nothing to do with hornets at all.

*****

"Hey, short and stupid!"

At the sound of that voice, Jacob tore out of the cafeteria and down the hall until he finally ducked into Mr. Lorenz's room.

Mr. L., as everyone called him, looked up from the pile of papers on his desk and pushed his glasses onto his forehead. "Jacob, what's going on? Weren't you just here last hour?"

Jacob moved closer to Mr. L.'s desk where he was less likely to be seen. "Yeah, I, uh, just wanted to ask when the science project was due."

He couldn't tell him he was simply there to avoid Willard, the biggest, nastiest kid in his class. Yet, he knew that if he stalled long enough in Mr. L.'s room, he could escape some of the pain Willard planned for him. He'd probably get more the next time he was caught, but after doing the math in his head, he concluded that missing out on one beating made up for it.

"It's due tomorrow." Mr. L. was actually answering his made up question. "I would hope you'd have already started. This assignment is not the kind of thing you can do well in a short time."

Jacob caught sight of the corner of the blackboard where the due date for the science project was clearly posted. "I, uh, sure. It's almo. . .almost. . .mostly done." He took a deep breath and stared at his feet. He wasn't about to admit that he hadn't even thought about the science project until this moment.

Mr. L. leaned forward and rested his chin on his hands. "So why are you here?"

"I wanted to see how much longer I had, you know, so I could make it as good as possible."

"Well, I'm glad you're taking it seriously. Like I said, you've got one more day. But for now, you'd better get to your next class before the bell rings."

"Thanks, Mr. L." Jacob stopped at the doorway and looked both ways. Seeing that the halls were empty, he started on his way.

"Hey, short and stupid, get over here!"

Jacob froze.

"Don't you dare run away."

Willard stood in the side hall that led to the band room. His long, dark hair had an extra coat of grease combed into it and the sleeves on his shirt were rolled up to show his "larger than anyone else in the school" biceps.

"I have to get to class," Jacob said, motioning down the hallway toward the classrooms ahead of him. It was a pitiful excuse that would never work.

"I said, come here, you little turd."

Willard would go over-the-top, crazy mad if he ran twice in a row. *Might as well get it over with.* As soon as Jacob was within striking distance, Willard punched him in the arm.

"Oww! What was that for?"

"You're supposed to stay put when I talk to you. Hold up your hands."

Jacob put his hands in the air with his palms open. Willard grabbed them, twisted Jacob's arms upside down and bent his fingers back farther than ever before. The knuckle burner dropped Jacob to his knees.

Spit flew out of Willard's mouth and onto Jacob's forehead as he made his next demand.

"Say it!"

"Say what?"

"You're gonna do what I want when I want it."

"I'll do what you want."

"Say it all."

Jacob's hands went numb as he pushed out the words, "when you want it."

"That's more like it." Satisfied with the results of his work, Willard released his grip and walked away, shaking his head. "What a dope."

Chapter Two – The Great Pine

Every time he got off the bus, Jacob thought about his mother's homemade rolls. She often made them in the early afternoon so warm treats would be waiting for him when he got home. He could picture it. He'd dump his backpack on the faded tile floor, tear open a roll, load it up with peanut butter and shove the whole gooey mess in his mouth. After washing it down with cold milk, he'd repeat the process till he was fully satisfied. But he wouldn't get to that kitchen or those rolls for a while since their gravel driveway was long and he was unusually slow when he wasn't running away from something.

Closer to the house, the driveway made a sharp left turn past a tall pine tree. As usual, he yanked a handful of needles from one of its lower branches and tossed them in the air. He stopped underneath the kitchen window to take a deep breath. He'd be able to smell freshly baked rolls if his mother had made them. *Aaah,* exactly what he'd hoped for.

But before he could take even one step toward those rolls, the earth beneath him shook and a deafening sound echoed through the yard. When he turned around to find out what was happening, chunks of mud hit him in the face.

He wiped the dirt from his eyes only to see the pine shake more mud off its roots and onto him.

Somehow the tree had ripped itself out of the ground. Now it stood just a few feet away and taller than ever. Jacob froze as the pine pounded its branches against its trunk like a gorilla claiming new territory.

His awe turned to terror when the Great Pine charged. For a split second, he couldn't imagine this was really happening. But with the tree almost on top of him, he knew what he had to do, what he always did when he was in trouble, what he did better than anyone. *Run! Run away! Run away now!*

He sprinted from one end of the yard to the other—across the driveway, around the picket fence, toward the chicken coop. He'd never gone faster. Yet, the tree stayed with him.

This is crazy. Trees can't run. Yet this one could. He needed to create some space between himself and the tree. Maybe if he raced around the house, he'd get ahead of it. He had to be able to take corners faster than a tree. So, around the house he went. Around and around they both went—five, six, seven times—as questions raced through his head.

Why is a tree chasing me?—and—*What will it do if it catches me?* He was sure no one outside of a lumberjack had ever been threatened by a tree the way he was at this moment. His lungs burned and his legs felt heavy. Yet the tree didn't stop, so neither could he.

While he pushed his body to keep going, his

mind struggled to come up with a new strategy. Then, it came to him. It was too simple. He'd go into the house. He'd open the door, duck inside and head to the basement.

The plan was both ingenious and comforting at the same time. He kept repeating it to assure himself he'd be okay as soon as he got in the house. *The tree is too big to go into the basement. The tree is too big to go into the basement. The tree is TOO BIG to go into the basement!*

He tore around each corner, two, three, four more times. As he took the last turn on his last lap, he grabbed the handle on the front door, swung it open and dove inside. The door slammed shut behind him as he pounded his feet against the basement steps. Once downstairs, he collapsed against an old table which sat in the middle of the room and sucked in all the oxygen he could. *I'll be safe in the basement. Trees don't come into basements.*

Except for this one! The Great Pine somehow forced its way in and was now standing across from him.

Stupid, stupid, stupid! He slapped his head. *A tree that can pull itself out of the ground to run on its roots can do anything. Why didn't I stay outside?*

Now, whether he went to the right or to the left or down to the floor, the tree could reach him. As the Great Pine drew back its largest branch, readying itself for a powerful blow, Jacob pictured his head crashing against the concrete. Blood and brains would be everywhere. He covered his face and screamed, "No!"

He expected to feel pine needles scraping against his skin. Instead, he felt a rush of energy and a warm, fuzzy blanket covering his face. When he pushed off the blanket, he saw the shelf his dad made. On it was his baseball glove and a video game he'd played the night before. He was back in his bedroom—back in the world where pine trees stay in the ground.

"Only a dream," he said to convince himself it wasn't real. Yet, his lungs hurt and the smell of pine in his nose reminded him that he'd had this dream many times before.

"Jacob, hurry up! The bus will be here soon," his mother called up the stairs. Of course! Her voice had brought him out of the dream just like the smell of the pancakes she was frying got him thinking about her homemade rolls.

He wanted to say, *Thanks for saving my life, Mom! Thanks for saving me from certain destruction!* Instead, he yelled, "I'll be there in a minute!"

"You don't have a minute. It's already ten after seven."

Late again, he jumped out of bed and picked yesterday's jeans off the floor. He grabbed a t-shirt off the banister and held it to his nose. *Good enough.* As he made his way down the thirteen steps to the living room, he pulled it over his head. With his arms in the air and his face partially covered, his feet slipped. His legs flew out from under him and his butt banged down on the last three steps. Whop! Whop! Whop!

"Smooth move." His sister Olivia stood in front of him with one hand on her hip. *"Why did she have to be right there?"*

"Shut up. It's not funny. It really hurts."

"Oooh, are your little butt cheeks sore?" She put her other hand over her mouth, but it wasn't enough to muffle her laughter completely.

Looking in from the kitchen, his mother asked, "Are you all right?"

"Yeah," he grunted.

In spite of their mom's concern, Olivia kept giggling. Well, if she wouldn't go away, he would. He got up and hobbled toward the kitchen, rubbing his backside.

"It's not fair to make fun of someone who's in pain," he loudly complained. "What if I broke my neck? What if I broke my neck and my body was paralyzed and the doctors couldn't fix me and I had to spend the rest of my life in a wheelchair?" He stopped in the doorway and pointed at Olivia. "And you'd have to take care of me. You'd even have to change my diapers! Wouldn't be so funny then, would it?"

His over the top description of what could have been even got a laugh out of his mother.

On his way out the door, he grabbed a pancake off the table. And as he passed the pine tree, he yelled, "You can leave me alone too, Mister 'I'm a pine tree and I can run.' Quit chasing me!"

Grumbling all the way to the road, he wondered which was worse—being stalked by a pine tree in a dream or teased by his sister once he woke up. Not able to decide, he gave himself plenty of sympathy for both.

Chapter Three – The Bus

As they waited for the bus at the end of the driveway, Olivia checked her hair for the thousandth time and put on one more coat of lip gloss. "Fresh paint job?" Jacob teased as he swallowed the last of his pancake.

"You don't know anything about women, do you?"

He shrugged and pictured something he cared about more at that moment than Olivia's opinion—closing his eyes for the forty-five minute ride to school. But when his backpack, loaded with books, started to slide off his shoulders, it hit him. *Crap! I forgot to do my homework.*

Just then, the doors of the bus crashed open in front of them. Olivia hopped on while Jacob used the handrail to pull himself up one painful step at a time.

At the top of the stairs, he stood next to the driver, who was settled into a brown, cushioned seat. It had to be the only comfortable place on the bus. An oversized mirror hung over the driver's head so he could keep tabs on everything behind him, although he never looked up. Jacob held tight to the silver railing which separated the driver from his passengers, for once he went past it, he'd cross into a world where the only way to be safe was to surround yourself with others who pretended to be just like you even if they weren't.

Closest to the front sat the nerds, who poured over the latest edition of their comic books. Right behind them were the kids who wanted to read and study. Next were the jocks. They acted as if nobody else was even on the bus—except when they checked out the popular girls across the aisle. They were busy sharing the latest about everything and everyone. Kids who talked extra loud in order to be noticed sat in the middle while anyone looking to cause trouble found their way to the back.

Jacob didn't have a group, but he did have his best friend, Tommy Leaver, who always saved him a seat. Though to get to it without trouble, he'd have to maneuver past three people who posed three different challenges.

First was Del Seliger, otherwise known as Smelly Delly. As Jacob made his way down the aisle, Del looked up at him with his bugged out eyes and made his usual offer, "You can sit here." Jacob focused on the emergency door in the rear of the bus, held his breath, and kept moving.

Next was Liz Elliott. She'd already spotted him. Jacob shuddered as he remembered the time she'd blocked the aisle with her legs. While he waited for her to move out of the way, she grabbed his jacket, pulled him into the seat, and sat uncomfortably close. The best he could do was stare straight ahead and pretend not to be embarrassed.

"Look, Lizzy has a boyfriend," the other kids

said at the time. They even chanted, "Give her a kiss! Give her a kiss!"

Their teasing was way worse than Olivia giggling at him for a few seconds this morning. If it happened again, his life would be over. No, he would not, could not sit by Liz Elliott any more than he would ever sit by Smelly Delly Seliger. He used what little energy he had to push past her.

That left Willard. With hopes that he was busy hassling someone else, Jacob rushed to his seat, climbed over Tommy and slumped down out of sight next to the window.

"Hey, short and stupid!"

He crouched even lower.

"I'm talkin' to you. Are ya deaf?" Willard shouted as he moved up from the back. "Or is the little baby scared?"

Willard reached over Tommy to crack Jacob on the head. "That's for you, dummy." Then he let loose with a most unpleasant laugh. Everyone nearby, except Tommy, laughed along if only to keep from becoming his next victim.

"Jerk." Jacob muttered.

"Did you say somethin'?" Willard hovered over him.

"No."

"You better not." Willard gave his head another crack before he walked back to his seat with his chest out.

"He is a jerk," Tommy said under his breath. "You okay?"

"Yeah. I've got a pretty hard head."

"Well, you look messed up to me, man. I think he scrambled your brains."

"Nah, I'm just tired."

"Were you playing Fortnite? You were, weren't you? Why didn't you call me?"

"I wasn't playing Fortnite."

"Oh, so were you up talkin' to Liz, huh?"

"Shut up."

"Hey, I was just throwin' it out there. Why are you gettin' so mad about it? Oh, cause it's true. Are you guys are in l-u-v-e luuuv?"

"Seriously? You can't even spell love? I had a bad dream, okay?"

"You had nightmares? Awesome! What happened?" Tommy moved his backpack to the floor and leaned in closer. "Were there werewolves, mutants, people with their guts hangin' out? Was it so gross you wanted to puke? Share, man!"

"It wasn't gross."

"There had to be somethin' cool."

"I don't know. A tree chased me and I thought it was going to kill me. It felt like it was really happening. Then I woke up."

"A tree chased you? That's it?" Tommy leaned back into his seat. "Man, you're weird...and you gotta get better nightmares. Otherwise, don't tell me about 'em—at all. And for your information, what happens in your dreams isn't real."

Chapter Four – Aldjor

Annoyed and tired, Jacob leaned his head against the window and stared at the weeds in the ditch. As the bus picked up speed, they moved past the weeds more quickly. As if in a trance, his eyes closed. Yet everyone was making so much noise, he couldn't get the sleep he craved.

He picked up his head, determined to give a dirty look to whomever on the bus was being so loud. But he wasn't on the bus anymore! He was at the highest section of a huge stadium, standing on a small platform with his back against the wall. And the noise which bothered his sleep was coming from people as they settled into their seats. *What the heck?*

Before he could figure out what was going on, the stadium lights dimmed. Spotlights glared down onto a large stage which held nothing but a single microphone on a single stand. The crowd became quiet, then, without warning, jumped to its feet and cheered wildly. At the top of the stadium, bright lights flashed on a jumbotron, giving the impression fireworks were going off.

Yet all Jacob saw was an old man walk out to stand by the mike. *This can't be what they're all worked up about.* Except for his orange suspenders, there wasn't anything special about this man in the middle of the stage. He was short and thin with gray hair and a wrinkled face. His ears were too big for his head and his knees were bent just enough to make Jacob wonder how he kept from tipping over.

Maybe he'll introduce the main event. No, this man in the middle of the stage was the main event.

As he spoke, Jacob kept track of the crowd's reaction. They'd listen for a while before suddenly standing up to whistle, scream and applaud. The man in the middle waited for them to settle down, then got out a few more words before they did it again. From his spot in the back, Jacob couldn't make out what was being said, but the crowd's pattern of sitting quietly then standing to cheer made him think there had to be something worth hearing. He stepped forward to find out.

"Every time you dare to be yourself," the man in the middle said, "you are being incredibly brave because no one is exactly like you. So, don't give up on yourself, no matter what happens to you or what anyone says about you."

Jacob liked what he heard so far. After all, he regularly gave up on himself. He leaned in to hear more.

"Raaaggh, raaaggh!"

Deep and guttural, this wretched sound was a cross between a dog coughing up vomit and a lion roaring in the jungle. It grated on his ears and gave him a queasy stomach all at the same time. And though the man in the middle kept talking, this growl was all Jacob could hear. Still, the crowd didn't seem to be bothered.

"Raaaggh, raaaggh!"

Jacob couldn't help but look in the direction the noise came from, though he soon wished he hadn't. For there, partway down the row, was a creature so repulsive it brought tears to his eyes. This disgusting beast had a body which was more wide than tall. Though it had plenty of muscles, lumps of fat came out of it in a variety of places. One hung off its left side, another rose from its stomach, still another stuck out from its back.

Like crab grass, patches of black, prickly hair stood straight out from each lump. Everywhere else the creature's skin was red and rough as if it had been scrapped against a tree. *Gross!* he thought, though he kept staring.

"You're lying! They're all useless scum. Raaaggh, raaaggh!"

The creature's hateful words drew Jacob's attention to its mouth and head, which were equally dreadful. It looked like a lump of fat had been forced down onto its shoulders by a great weight. A misshaped wart grew out of one cheek. A clump of hair rose out of the other. A bristly snout completed its angry expression, a perfect match for the words which came out of it.

"Go back where you came from! You can't help these losers. They're pathetic. And so are you."

What is this thing?

With a smirk on its face, its head turned toward him. And though this time its mouth did not open, Jacob could hear its objection and feel its outrage.

"I'm not a thing. My name is Aldjor, one of the greatest Haggeldies you'll ever see. Don't I look magnificent, Jacob?"

It knew his name and was in his head! In that moment, he understood. Whether the creature spoke out loud or not, its words were going straight into his mind and his mind alone. No one else was upset by the Haggeldie's grumbling because no one else heard it. Did they even see this thing?

"Don't worry. If I wanted them to know I was here, they would."

Jacob took a step backwards and stared straight ahead. Maybe the Haggeldie would focus on harassing the man in the middle and leave him out of it if he kept a low profile. But Aldjor's head swiveled on its short, fat neck keeping him in its line of sight.

"What's wrong with you, Jacob, is that you're a giant screw up. No matter how well you do something, you always find a way to screw it up in the end."

Jacob looked to his left and his right for a side door, an emergency exit, any way to escape. But he was boxed in by rows of cheering people.

Aldjor laughed, "You can't get away from me." Then, he kept up the assault. "No one likes you and no one wants to be around you. You say the stupidest things and you're always feeling sorry for yourself. You're such a loser. Why don't you just give up on yourself already?"

Maybe he's right.

Aldjor was quick to respond. "I am right. You're as awful as anything."

Was it possible this nauseating beast spoke the truth—things everyone else was too polite to tell him? He did mess up a lot, and he didn't fit in with other kids. The more Aldjor spoke, the lower Jacob hung his head. Finally, he gave in to the Haggeldie's description of him and to all the bad feelings that went with it.

Aldjor ended the attack by digging a bony finger into Jacob's chest and yelling, "Get out of here! Go on. Get out of here." He was so repulsed by the Haggeldie's touch, his body shook, which woke him up.

He was back on the bus. And Smelly Delly was in his face, poking him and yelling, "Wake up, Jacob. We're at school. We have to get out of here."

It was only a dream—a disgusting, disturbing, dreadful dream, to be sure, but only a dream. Aldjor was gone and he was safe, though he could still feel the sting of the Haggeldie's words.

He rubbed his eyes, grabbed his backpack and gave Del the "thank you" his mother would expect.

"Come on, we have to get going," Smelly Delly

said.

What "we"? There is no "we."

He made sure to stay a few steps behind Del as they headed into school. And for his whole first hour class, he couldn't stop thinking about the Haggeldie. It seemed real enough to touch, as real as the air moving past his face when the pine tree swung its branch at him. Was it all his imagination? Was he in real danger either time? Maybe Tommy was right. Maybe he was weird and made too much of dreams everybody had. Still, he couldn't get the images of terrifying trees and horrifying Haggeldies out of his head.

Chapter Five – The Man in the Middle

The math test! *Crap!* He totally forgot about the math test. Could he somehow study during his other classes? *Second hour social studies, no problem. Third hour Spanish, no problem. Fourth hour science, double crap!*

His science project was due today and he hadn't even started. How was he supposed to make a volcano that would send up smoke and shoot out lava by fourth hour plus study for the math test?

"Students will proceed to the auditorium at the end of third hour for a special all-school assembly which will replace our fourth hour classes," the principal announced over the intercom.

Yes! He pumped his arm. School assemblies were lame, but this one would get him out of science and give him time to study, if he ignored the speaker.

As usual, he was one of the last ones to get to the auditorium.

"Hey, man. You finally made it." Tommy was waiting for him.

"Yeah, I did. And by the way, thanks for leaving me on the bus with Smelly Delly."

"I figured you didn't want me to wake you up from another one of your boring dreams," Tommy grinned. "Where are we gonna sit?"

"I'm going to sit far away from you. I have to study for a math test."

"Okay, but don't get too smart or I'll have to find a new friend."

"Ha ha," Jacob replied.

He found a place near kids he didn't know while the principal rambled on. "We have with us today Dr. John L. Malson, who will speak about. . ."

Blah, blah, blah. Jacob congratulated himself for not having his homework done. Doing it during an assembly would be way better than listening to some dull doctor. He made notes about using wood alcohol, marshmallow crème and fire to make his science project happen. He only glanced up while he was getting out his math book. *Wait, no. . .it can't be.*

There, at the podium, stood a man who was short and thin, with gray hair and a wrinkled face. His ears were too big for his head and his knees were bent just enough to make Jacob wonder how he kept from tipping over. More remarkable than that, he was wearing orange suspenders.

"The man in the middle," he said out loud.

One of the older kids mocked him. "Duh, you figured out he's a man and he's in the middle of the stage. Way to go, dork." Others laughed.

But in that moment, he didn't care how stupid he sounded or how much they made fun of him.

During the rest of the assembly, he stared at the doctor and tried to figure it out, *How did this guy end up in my dream? Did I ever see him before? Was his picture in the paper? Did my parents take me to him when I was little? It's crazy.* When the assembly was over, he rushed to the front to find out if the doctor knew him.

"Thanks for being here today," the principal said. "Students always need positive messages."

"Happy to do it," the doctor replied and started off stage.

Jacob was ready with his questions when Dr. John L. Malson looked him straight in the eye and winked. It was the kind of wink you give someone when you share a secret.

What was that? Was he just being friendly? Was he letting me know he knew about my dream? That's too strange. But why did he look at me that way?

The rest of the day, he did his best to ignore his teachers and study for the math test, but he couldn't stop thinking about Dr. Malson and the man in the middle. That night after supper, he went online. Maybe some website would explain how his dreams had gotten so tangled together with his everyday life. Nine hundred twenty-seven million websites popped up, each one promising to reveal the meaning behind any dream a person could have. Yet none described what he'd been through.

"You're working awfully late. Do you have a lot

of homework tonight?"

"Oh, hi, Mom." He hadn't heard her come into the room. "Yeah, I guess. A bunch of stuff for science." True enough. He just wasn't working on it.

"Well, don't stay up too much longer. You know how hard it is for you to get up in the morning." She leaned against the doorframe and smiled.

"I won't."

Two more hours and a whole lot of web pages later, he had zero answers. He laid his head on the desk and closed his eyes. *"Just a short break."*

Within seconds, he was standing in an open field. The sun shone down from an endless blue sky and warmed his face. Jacob breathed in the sweet smell of fresh cut hay and looked around. To his left was a road. To his right was wild grass. Straight ahead was a fence. And next to the fence was a ginormous rock. At least twelve feet around, the rock rose more than six feet out of the ground. He had to climb it.

Once on top, he checked out the neighboring farm where a red tractor was parked by the barn. Cows grazed in the pasture. A golden retriever laid on the grass. When he turned to his left, he saw someone standing on the road. At first he thought it might be the farmer, except no farmer ever wore orange suspenders.

He jumped off the rock and raced to the road where he came face-to-face with Dr. John L.

Malson, who held out his hand and winked once again.

"It's good to see you, Jacob."

"You know who I am?" His eyes got wide.

"Of course. I saw you in the crowd."

"I came up to the stage to ask you some stuff, but you were talking to the principal."

"Oh, at school today. Yes, yes I saw you there as well. I meant when you were up on the platform, when the Haggeldie complained about you—and about me."

"It was you there."

"Yes, it was."

"And that thing really is called a Haggeldie? I thought I imagined it."

"Unfortunately, it's real."

"It was ugly and gross and mean!"

"Gross for sure."

"Mr. Malson. . .I mean, Dr. Malson, how could you see me way up there? It was dark."

"I see more than you'd expect. By the way, here I'm not Mr. Malson or Dr. Malson."

"But the principal said you were Doctor John L. Malson."

"True. In the place you saw me today my name is John L. Malson and I am a doctor. Here I'm something more."

"Oh, I get it. Here you're the man in the middle."

"You first saw me in the middle of the stage, didn't you?" He chuckled. "I guess the title fits since I am sort of in the middle of everything around here."

He stared into the eyes of the Man in the Middle and saw someone who was much stronger on the inside than he appeared to be on the outside.

"You do look different here."

"Everyone looks different here. Even you."

Dozens of mirrors instantly rose out of the ground creating a wall around them. Jacob's image was reflected back at him a hundred times. No matter where he looked, he saw himself, unless he looked down, which is what he did.

"I'm sure you'd rather watch the grass grow than look at yourself. Yet, this is a rare opportunity to see who you really are. Take it. Look into the mirrors."

He couldn't imagine why he would. He didn't like what he saw in the bathroom mirror at home. His nose was crooked, his ears stuck out, and his forehead was covered with pimples. Looking more closely at himself sounded like a really bad idea. Yet, the Man in the Middle insisted.

"You want answers, don't you? Well, before you can learn the truth about me or this place, you need to begin to face the truth about yourself."

Slowly, he lifted his head. At first, he only saw the twelve-year-old boy he always saw. Though after a while, he noticed something different. The boy in the mirrors stood taller and stared out ahead of himself as if he were looking into the future or headed out on an adventure.

"The look on your face tells me you're seeing something you hadn't anticipated. Good. Just don't be fooled. These mirrors only reveal what is already true. You're more than you think you are. We all are, even if we don't always see it. Excellent start."

"Yeah, sure. But none of this stuff is real. This field isn't real. The Haggeldie wasn't real. You're not real. And what I saw in the mirrors isn't real either, so it doesn't matter. It's all just a dream."

The Man in the Middle squeezed his face and laughed. "Feels real to me."

Once again, Jacob stared at the ground. "Sorry."

"It's okay, Jacob. This is a lot to absorb. But the truth is that your dreams are not just dreams. They're a gateway to the world of Chimeran."

"The world of Chimeran?"

"Exactly. Look around you," the Man in the Middle said as the mirrors slid back into the earth. "This is the world of Chimeran, which is as real as the world you live in every day."

Jacob looked back toward the rock and the fence line. "If Chimeran is a whole world, why do I just see a boring old field?"

"A boring old field is something you're familiar with, which makes it the perfect place for you to begin exploring Chimeran."

"Why would I want to do that?"

"Because Chimeran is so much more than you can imagine. It's a place where you can discover what you are worth—it's a world where you can find courage. But enough questions. Whatever else you need to know will be revealed to you in time. For now, you'll have to live without all the answers—and trust me instead. And trust that being who you are is enough."

With that, the Man in the Middle walked away.

"Will I see you again?" Jacob shouted after him.

"Many times, I'm sure."

"If this is Chimeran, then what do you call the place where I live the rest of my life?"

The Man in the Middle stopped and shook his head. "You can't help yourself, can you? Okay, what you think of as your only reality, the place you live from day to day, here we call it Telluris."

"Telluris," he repeated as the Man in the Middle disappeared from sight. He didn't understand everything he'd been told, but he began to think he just might not be crazy.

Chapter Six – Another Day in Paradise

Mr. Kinderman, the one and only gym teacher at Lakeside School, shouted his orders from the other end of the gym. "Guys, get down here as fast as you can. We've got a lot to get done. Today, you'll be playing volleyball. Now, it's not just about having fun. I want you to learn how to work together—as a team, because in the game of volleyball, as in the game of life, you win or lose as a team. Okay, Randy, Karl, you're our captains. Randy, you pick first."

"I'll take Willard."

Of course, he took Willard. He was always the first one taken because he was the tallest, strongest kid in class, which happens when you're held back two grades. Plus, if he was on your side, he'd pick on the other team instead of you.

Jacob began to count the number of holes his shoelaces went through on his new Reeboks as he waited. His name wouldn't be called for a long time. Not that he was a bad volleyball player. He could dig the ball out and set it up as well as anybody. He was just too short to reach over the net.

His only comfort was that he wouldn't be chosen last. That honor was reserved for Smelly Delly or Justin Jamerson, whose left leg was two inches shorter than his right one. Still, being picked ahead of them was nothing to brag about.

Today, Willard and Jacob ended up on opposite teams. Unfortunately, they also lined up directly across from each other at the net.

Willard's team scored first off one of his spikes. . .then again. . .and again. They set it up for him as often as possible, and each time, he hit a winner—right at Jacob. The game was turning into a slaughter.

"Hey, short and stupid," Willard whispered. "I'm gonna knock you on your butt with the next one. You'll end up dopier than ever."

Jacob said nothing.

Willard's next spike barely missed his head. "Pretty good, ain't I?"

Again, Jacob said nothing.

Every shot flew past him so quickly he didn't have time to react. Six nothing, seven nothing.

"We're gonna skunk you so bad you'll stink worse than Smelly Delly," Willard bragged.

Still, Jacob said nothing. And in spite of Willard's prediction, Jacob's team did finally score. But they lost the serve right afterwards.

"Hey, coach." A secretary from the main office opened the gym door. "You've got a phone call."

"Guys, I have to take this. Keep things going until I get back." Then, he looked each player in the eyes. "Two things," he said in a serious tone. "Play by the rules and no screwing around!"

Soon the score was nine to one. The next

serve floated high in the air toward Jacob, who was ready to send it to the other team's back line when Willard reached under the net and shoved him. The ball hit Jacob's knee and dribbled out of bounds.

"Why don't you hit it over to our side once in a while, numb nuts?" Willard snorted.

"I would if you'd stop pushing me!" The words flew out of his mouth. *Why did he yell at Willard? Everyone knew not to yell at Willard.* In an instant, Willard put his hands around his neck and shoved him up against the stage.

"What did you say?" The edge of the stage dug into his back. "Say it to my face, tough guy. Tell me it's my fault you suck. Otherwise, you better take it back."

He would gladly take back what he'd said along with anything else Willard might have thought he said, even if he hadn't said it. But Willard's grip on his throat was so tight he couldn't.

"Hey, break it up! Willard, let him go." Mr. Kinderman was back. Willard gave Jacob's neck one last squeeze, put both his hands in the air and stepped away as if he were innocent. Jacob coughed to clear his throat.

"I told you guys, no screwing around. Willard, I want to see you in my office right after class. Everybody, get back to the game."

"Yes, Mr. Kinderman." Willard turned back toward Jacob and mouthed, "I'll catch you later."

The rest of the day, he kept an eye out for Willard, expecting to be ambushed in the hallway or attacked while getting something out of his locker.

"Hey, man." Tommy caught up to him on the way to their next class. "What's up?"

"Willard's out to get me." Then he explained what happened.

On the ride home, Jacob sat right behind the bus driver. Tommy plopped down beside him. "Playin' it safe?"

"Yup."

"Works for me," Tommy said.

The next morning, Jacob sat there again and got off the bus as soon as he could. But before he made it into the school, Willard grabbed him by the collar and dragged him around the corner of the building.

"Did you think you were gonna get away with it?"

"Get away with what?"

"Callin' me out in front of everybody."

"But I didn't do anything."

Willard threw Jacob's backpack to the ground and pushed him backwards till he crashed into the wall, which knocked the wind out of him. Then Willard smothered him with his large body and bellowed into his ear. "When I decide to push somebody, I push 'em hard. And I never cheat 'cause I'm that good. Remember it, ya little queer."

As Willard walked away, Jacob gasped for air and collected his backpack, all the while repeating, "Don't ever say anything to make Willard mad. Don't ever say anything to make Willard mad."

Chapter Seven – Preparing for Battle

Jacob fell asleep that night thinking about the rock in the fence line, and before he knew it, he found himself in the middle of the field in Chimeran. Within seconds, he was on top of that rock, searching for the Man in the Middle. Whether Chimeran was real or not, maybe the Man in the Middle could help him figure out how to stand up to Willard.

When Jacob couldn't find him by the road or at the farm, he looked toward the other end of the field where there'd been wild grass. In its place was a woods. And in the front of the woods was a cave. And outside the entrance to the cave was a girl. *Where did all that come from. . .where did she come from?*

As he moved across the field to investigate, he checked her out. The girl wore a chest protector made of leather and metal along with leather boots and a metal helmet. On her back was a circle of feathers. She looked like a fierce warrior.

She stood like one, too—with her left foot behind her and her right foot in front. Holding a sword in one hand and a shield in the other, she moved with ease as she attacked an imaginary foe. And every time she stepped forward, she let out a cry. "Aieee!"

The size of her scream and the power behind

her every move startled him. He got so caught up in watching her, he didn't realize how close he was getting or how fast he was going—until he tripped over a stump, tumbled forward and landed on the ground right behind her. She turned on him in a flash, her sword flying over his body. "Aieee!"

He crossed his arms over his chest to keep from being stabbed in the heart. The girl screamed a second time, pulled her sword back and stepped away. But it was too late. His arm had been cut.

"What are you doing? Who sneaks up on someone who's got a sword? I could have really hurt you."

"What am I doing? What. . .what are you doing? You almost killed me. And by the way, I am hurt—bad! Look where you cut me."

She leaned in to look at his arm. "Don't be a crybaby. It's only a scratch. Besides, I didn't mean to hurt you. I didn't even see you there! You shouldn't have come up behind me like that."

"You think it's my fault for being cut by your sword? My fault for you swinging a sword around like a crazy person? Really?"

The warrior girl took a deep breath and returned to what she'd been doing. Meanwhile, he paced back and forth, staring at the cut and mumbling. "She should be more careful. She could've killed me. Look at the blood on my arm. There's something seriously wrong with her."

The longer he mumbled, the louder he got till the girl could hear every one of his accusations. He stopped talking when she turned in his direction, but it was too late. She'd already shoved her sword in the ground and was headed his way.

"Let me have a look." A scab had already formed over the tiny cut. "I told you, it's nothing."

"Nothing? You think it's nothing? You. . .you're nothing! You should pay more attention to what's happening around you."

She shook her head and went back to her swordplay. Since his complaints didn't gain any sympathy, he stopped to watch her make-believe battle. *She may be a psycho, but she's really good with a sword.* He wasn't going to tell her, of course. Still, he wondered what she was doing in a woods in front of a cave. It was hardly the normal place for a sword fighter.

"How come you have a sword? Are you playing war or something?"

She kept going through her moves. "I'm not playing anything. I am training."

"What's with all the yelling?"

"It shows my enemies that I'm strong and they had better watch out." Advancing on no one, she let out another cry. "Aieee."

"You have enemies? Who are they? All the people you cut before?" As soon as he said it, he knew he shouldn't have. Smart remarks had gotten him in trouble in the past. And this girl had a sword.

She jammed that sword into the ground once more and came straight at him. He gulped, retreated a few steps and considered apologizing, not because he might have hurt her feelings, but because she might hurt him. At least she hadn't brought her weapon along.

When they were nose to nose, she whispered, "Yes, I do have many enemies, dangerous enemies—the same way you do. And I have cut them with my sword."

His body shivered. She placed her forehead against his and looked straight into his eyes. "I'm not sure when they'll show up, but they've come after me before, and they'll come after me again. I plan to be ready for them." With that, she returned to her preparation.

Suddenly he didn't care about winning an argument. He was only concerned with one thing. She said he had enemies. Lots of people bugged him to some extent, yet he wouldn't call them enemies—not even Willard. Besides, Willard told him that whatever he did to him was his own fault.

Having thought it through a good ten seconds, he approached her again, though he moved slower and stayed farther away to avoid getting stabbed. "You're wrong. I have maybe one enemy, maybe, and even he wouldn't stick me with a sword."

She gave him the same stern look he got from

his teachers when he hadn't tried hard enough. "Your enemies are out there. Maybe you know them, maybe you don't. No matter. They want to hurt you, just like mine want to hurt me. And they will use anything to attack you—a sword, words, your feelings, anything. But make no mistake. You do have enemies, and they will come after you."

More questions popped into his head: How many enemies did he have, would they all come after him at the same time, would he be able to run from them? Still, he only asked one. "How could they use my feelings to attack me? It doesn't make any sense."

"Aaah!" She rolled her eyes. "Do you pay any attention at all to what you are feeling?"

"I dunno."

"Look, people have all sorts of feelings, and they're not all good. Like fear. Who doesn't get afraid? But when we choose to be afraid rather than brave, our fear becomes a weapon for our enemies."

"I don't get it."

"Okay, what if your enemies can make you worry about what bad thing is going to happen next? They could keep you from being happy."

Every day, he wondered what might go wrong. And other people did seem happier than he was. Still, even if his enemies used fear and worry as weapons, he couldn't fight back with a sword. Before he could make his point, though, she spoke again.

"Aren't there people who make sure to tell you what's wrong with you?"

"All the time."

"It's hard to be around them, right?"

He nodded. "One kid always calls me names."

"Well, him and people like him use what you already think about yourself to make you feel bad. I bet I could name the most powerful weapon your enemies use against you."

He stuck his chin out and stood as tall as possible. "I'll bet you can't."

"You like to feel sorry for yourself."

"No I don't."

"Then why do you hang your head so much?"

"I don't hang my head." He pushed his chin up even higher.

"You hang your head like a sad little puppy."

"O yeah? Well, so what? Puppies are cute."

"Yes, but anybody can see how rotten you already feel and use it against you."

He took his time before asking his next question. "Okay, what if sometimes, maybe, I do feel sorry for myself. How exactly could they use it against me?"

"Well, when you look that sad they figure you won't stand up for yourself, so they don't think twice about pushing you around."

He bit his lip and turned away.

"I'm not trying to make you feel worse than you do. But sometimes you have to say or do something—anything—to show the world you're there."

How does she know all this about me?

"Don't worry. No one is totally happy with themselves. But our enemies will use those bad feelings against us at some point."

He looked back at her and asked, "Who are your enemies, really? You never said."

"I don't like to talk about them. I'd rather get ready to defeat them. Hey, would you like to help?"

"I dunno."

"Come on. We'll practice destroying our enemies." She swung her sword around as if cutting off someone's head, then stepped forward and stuck her sword into the earth where the unseen enemy had fallen. "There," she announced triumphantly, "you will never defeat me again!"

He envied this warrior girl because she'd do anything to defend herself against anyone who tried to hurt her—an option he'd never considered.

"Are you going to help me or not? I promise not to cut you—again. Just grab a sword."

She smiled and pointed in the direction of the cave where a silver sword with a bronze handle was leaning against the entrance. Taking a deep breath, he slowly went over to pick it up. It was so heavy, he wondered if he'd even be able to swing it.

"I've never been in a sword fight before, you

know. I've never even held a sword before. I'm sure I won't be much of a challenge for you."

"It's all right," she answered. "All you have to do is be my target."

Great!

In no time, the girl swung her sword at him with both precision and purpose. He swung his wildly, hoping to somehow block her blows, slow down her advances or knock the weapon out of her hand. None of his tactics worked. And whenever their weapons did crash against each other, his arm tingled and his sword went flying.

Most of the time, he ended up on the ground with her standing over him shouting her victory cry, "Aieee! Aieee!" But, without fail, she'd extend her arm and help him back up before attacking again.

This stinks. I'm losing. . .to a girl! I need to get out of here. Yet because she kept attacking, he had to keep fighting back and getting back up every time she knocked him down.

Forcing himself off the ground one last time, he begged his way out of more training. "You're really, really good. You'll do great against all your enemies, but I have got to get home, you know?" He rattled on, hoping one of his excuses would satisfy her. Whether she bought any of them or not, she let him off the hook.

"Thanks for helping. What's your name?"

"Jacob. . .Jacob Tannin. How about you?"

"Andrea Crantz."

"Well, good to meet you, Andrea. And good luck in the future—with all your battles and stuff."

"Good luck with yours. Will I see you again?"

"Yeah, sure."

He didn't mean it. He hoped to never run into her again, anywhere or anytime. Yet if he left on good terms, he might not become one of her enemies.

He went back to the fence line and crouched behind the stone. He wrapped his arms around himself and let the heat from the boulder comfort him. It had been a long time since he'd been able to feel sorry for himself, and it felt good. He closed his eyes and wished with all his might.

I want to be home. I don't want to fight any enemies. I don't want to face any challenges. I just want to wake up in my own room, which he did a few seconds later.

His body was sore. And his arm had a scab in the same place where the warrior girl had cut him. This confirmed it. Chimeran was a real place and not just a dream. Jacob was determined to go back to the field as soon as he could. He was just as determined to avoid Andrea when he got there.

Chapter Eight – The Brave Warrior

Chink! Chink! The sound of metal crashing against metal forced his eyes open. The last thing he remembered was being on his bed, watching TV. He must have fallen asleep because now he was leaning against the rock in Chimeran.

He sat up, rubbed the soreness out of his shoulder and peered around the rock. He could see dirt flying and swords flashing near the cave. This was a real life battle, nothing like the show he'd been watching. And he was certain Andrea wasn't involved since, even with all the shouting and howling, no one was screaming, "Aieee!"

He crept along the fence line till he got close enough to see who was part of this fight. Four Haggeldies surrounded one boy who looked to be about his age. They attacked him from every angle, but the boy fought back. He kicked one in the head, slashed another with his sword and jumped out of the way whenever necessary. Throughout the battle, the Haggeldies also screamed insults at him.

"Rones, you're worthless."

"You're weak."

"Look at his stupid head."

"You'll never beat us."

The boy pushed his dark hair out of his face and shouted back, "I am not what you say I am! And I will defeat you."

"You're exactly what we say you are. . .a sad, sorry loser nobody likes."

"You're liars. I have friends who would fight with me."

"Well, your imaginary friends aren't here. You're all alone."

Then they began their chant. "Rones is alone—Rones is alone—Rones is alone!" Their taunting didn't slow him down, though, as he defended himself against their swords and their words.

The more Jacob saw, the more impressed he was with the way the boy fought and the more he disliked Haggeldies. For a second, he considered helping, but quickly came up with several reasons why he shouldn't. First, it wasn't his fight. Second, he didn't have a sword. Third, he wasn't any good at fighting anyway. Besides, the boy and the Haggeldies were so involved with each other they never even noticed he was there.

Rones began to gain an advantage over the group by attacking one Haggeldie at a time. He'd chase it down and scream in its face, "I'm not what you say I am! Be gone!"

The defeated Haggeldie would run away shrieking. Yet before it was out of sight, it would yell, "I'll be back for you!" or "This isn't over!"

After he ran off the last of them, the boy did a victory dance. "Yes! I'm not who they say I am! It was all lies." Eventually, his dancing turned him in Jacob's direction. With an ear-to-ear grin and brown eyes that shone from his victory, the boy took a royal bow. "Greetings from Caldwell Rones, winner over every Haggeldie in sight. And who are you?"

"Oh, uh, I'm Jacob. Wow, I can't believe what you just did. That was awesome."

"It was pretty cool, wasn't it?"

"Have you fought Haggeldies before?"

"A few times."

"Do you always win?"

He laughed. "No, it doesn't work like that."

"How come you won today?"

Flexing his well-toned muscles, he bragged, "I train hard, like, all the time. Just look at these guns." They both laughed as he strutted.

"Seriously, I do train a lot because the Haggeldies never go away. I can either give in to them or find a way to defeat them. I choose to find a way to defeat them."

"They never go away?"

"It'll make more sense when it's your turn."

Jacob's stomach churned at the thought of battling Haggeldies. He backed away from the woods, looking in every direction. "What do you mean, 'my turn'? Are they coming after me next?"

"Not those Haggeldies. They only come after me. You have your own."

"I have my own Haggeldies?"

"Everybody does," Caldwell gave a slight shrug, as if it were no big deal. "Yours care most about hurting you."

"Why would they want to hurt me? I haven't done anything to them. I didn't even realize there were Haggeldies till a few days ago."

Caldwell pulled a rag out of his back pocket and wiped down the blade of his sword. "They don't want to hurt you because you did something to them. They want to hurt you because it makes them feel better. They'll come after you any chance they get."

Jacob checked the woods one more time. "How many do I have? Will they show up soon? Is there some place I can hide?"

"You're asking way too many questions. What really matters is if you can fight."

"What?"

"Do you know how to fight?"

Jacob flashed back to a recess when he got into it with Bennie, who was a grade younger and six inches shorter. They fought over who would be captain of their baseball team. Jacob thought he should since he was older. Bennie thought he should because he was a better player. Within seconds they were on the ground. It ended with Bennie sitting on top of him. The whole thing was painful and embarrassing, especially since everyone at school saw it.

So in his only fight, he was beaten by someone younger and smaller. He hung his head. "No, I don't."

"Want to learn?"

His head popped back up. "Yes!"

Caldwell put the rag away and held his sword up to the light. "Perfect." Placing the sword in its scabbard, he began Jacob's lessons. "First, never punch a Haggeldie in one of those lumps of fat. They won't feel it. And no matter how much you want to, never grab the hair growing out of those lumps. I found out real quick, it'll cut you in a thousand places. They use their hair as a weapon—to make you bleed."

Jacob winced. Then, Caldwell shared the most effective strategy of all. "The most important thing you can do is attack their weakness."

"What's their weakness?"

"The true weakness of every Haggeldie is your bravery."

His heart sank. He'd never been brave. Instead of admitting he was scared almost all the time, he asked, "How can you attack someone with your bravery?"

"Okay, look, what do Haggeldies do? They complain. They tell you everything that's wrong with you. They laugh at you for the way you look. They call you names like idiot, dummy. . ."

Jacob jumped in, "Freak, stupid, loser . . ."

"Exactly. I mean, you heard all the things they said about me. How I'm a loser and everyone hates me?"

"Couldn't miss it."

"They were just using the things I'm afraid of to make me feel bad about myself."

Jacob raised his eyebrows. "You think you're

a loser and everybody hates you?"

"Sometimes," Caldwell admitted. "They just said it out loud to get to me. Words have power. But here's the secret. My words have power, too."

"What do you mean?"

"My words hurt them as much as their words hurt me. Hey, everybody's words have power."

"Not mine," Jacob said.

"Your words are the strongest weapon you have. Your words show the Haggeldies how brave you are and that you don't believe what they're saying about you. Every time you speak up for yourself, your bravery becomes a weapon and they get closer to giving up."

"Is that why you argued against everything they said?"

"It's the best way to stop them. But you have to say what you believe and believe what you say—especially about yourself. Otherwise, your words have no power and you'll believe what they say. You'll lose for sure, then."

Caldwell's last piece of advice seemed the hardest of all as he thought about what Aldjor said to him at the stadium. "You'll always find a way to mess things up." How could he yell back, "Not true!" when he believed it was?

Jacob gave his head a quick shake to force the question out of his mind. He needed to concentrate on the fighting, which would cause him enough trouble.

"How am I going to learn all this? I'm no good

with my fists or my feet. I don't even own a sword. And I don't think I could talk while I'm fighting."

"Practice hard enough and you'll get the hang of it. Besides, you did okay against Andrea."

"You saw us? Where were you? Why didn't I see you? Why were you spying on us?"

"Wow, you ask a lot of questions."

"Sorry, I. . .I can't slow my brain down sometimes. I was just surprised you were there."

"In Chimeran, you never know who's watching. It might be a friend or it might be an enemy. So you have to be ready—because Haggeldies could attack at any time. Enough talking—let's practice."

"Could you answer one question first?"

"Sure."

"Does she scare you?"

Caldwell laughed. "Andrea? No. You get used to her. Now, let's do this!"

As quickly as he said, "Let's do this," he pounced on Jacob, threw him to the ground and sat on his stomach. It took about as long as it had taken Bennie to win the schoolyard fight, except Caldwell did more than sit on him. He also shouted at him. "You're the worst fighter I've ever seen! You'll never defeat any Haggeldies! I can't make a warrior out of you."

"Get off!" Jacob moaned. "It hurts. Why are you being so mean?"

"Whining's not going to help. You have to speak up for yourself. The Haggeldies will jump all over you and tear you apart with their words like I did. What are you going to say?"

He pursed his lips, took several quick breaths, then blurted out. "You're wrong. I'm not a loser, and I will find a way to defeat my enemies."

"You actually said something," Caldwell exclaimed as he climbed off Jacob's stomach. "It's the first step in becoming a brave warrior. Let's do it again."

As soon as Jacob got to his feet, Caldwell came at him. And for the rest of the afternoon, Jacob experimented with different ways to defend himself against Caldwell's attacks.

When they'd done all they could, Caldwell rested his hand on Jacob's shoulder. "You're doing way better than when we started. Now let's go to the cave."

Caldwell led him down more than twenty steps into a large, open space where a domed ceiling rose high above them. Rocks the size of big black bears were scattered across the back wall and a campfire burned in the middle of the cave.

"Have a seat." Caldwell pointed to the logs which circled the fire. "I'll fix you a warrior's meal."

"I don't feel like a warrior."

"Hey, you just started."

After scarfing down every bit of the food Caldwell made, they lay on the floor to rest. Jacob was tired, but in a good way, because for the first time in his life, he stood up for himself.

It didn't take long for him to fall asleep. And as soon as he fell asleep in the cave, he woke up in his bedroom, in the world of home and school. He got dressed and went downstairs long before his mother had to warn him about being late. He even walked into the kitchen with a smile on his face.

"What's for breakfast?"

His mother looked him over, "Well, well, you're dressed and ready to go. This is something new."

As he sat at the kitchen table, he thought, *Yes, it is.*

Chapter Nine – Bologna Surprise

With a glum look on his face, Jacob stared at the sandwich on his tray. *What sadistic lunch lady came up with the bologna surprise? And why did she do it?* Was it part of a contest to see who could produce the most tasteless, disgusting sandwich in the history of the universe? Did someone invent it to cause students unspeakable suffering? Either way, the bologna surprise is one sick sandwich.

First, two slices of bologna are placed inside a hamburger bun. Then, it's roasted till both the top and bottom of the bun are burnt, as are the edges of the bologna. Once the sandwich comes out of the oven, it sits on the counter till it's both cold and dry before it's handed to the students. No butter, mayo, or mustard is ever added, ensuring it is not spoiled by flavor of any kind.

He'd probably never find out who created the bologna surprise, but he understood the surprise part of its name. Surprise, Jacob, this is what you're eating today because you forgot to pack your own lunch! Surprise, Jacob's stomach, here's a little something you'll have a hard time keeping down.

It was this or nothing. He carefully tore off the darkest sections of the bun until only the soft, white insides were left. He peeled back the burnt edges of the bologna as well and set them in another compartment of his tray. Once he salvaged what he could, he sighed and began the struggle of swallowing what was left. Lots of chocolate milk would be needed to get this bad boy down.

"I hate this stuff." Tommy sat across from him, as usual. If it weren't for Tommy, he'd eat all by himself every day.

"Yours looks worse than mine."

"I'm so hungry. I'd eat anything," Tommy said, although it came out as "I'm tho hungy I'dee adyhin" since he'd just taken a huge bite of his sandwich. Jacob laughed, causing a mixture of bun, bologna and chocolate milk to fly out of his mouth onto Tommy's tray. Even that didn't keep Tommy from taking another bite.

"Goss, man, kee tha to ursef," Tommy protested. Jacob laughed even harder, causing him to spit out most of what was left in his mouth. Still, he didn't feel like he was wasting food because a bologna surprise didn't belong in the food category.

Whap! A hand slapped the back of his head. He didn't have to look up to know who it was. "Hey, short and stupid, what ya laughin about?"

When Jacob didn't answer right away, Willard cuffed him again and moved to the end of the table. "Come on, share—what's so funny?"

What can I say to make him quit bugging us? What would Caldwell say? "Tommy's talking with food in his mouth. But that doesn't give you the right to hit us. Why don't you leave us alone?"

"Not till you show me, goat face."

Tommy took another bite and said, "Thee, I cand dalk vewy well."

"That's not funny. That's just stupid. You guys are idiots." Willard mashed up what was left of the food in their tray and slapped them both on the head. "Now that's funny."

As Willard walked away, Jacob took a drink of milk and shook his head. His words hadn't changed a thing. Tommy scraped together what was left of his bologna surprise and shoved it in his mouth.

"I hate him," Tommy said. Only this time the words came out clearly and Jacob didn't laugh at all.

Chapter Ten – First Blood

Hoping to get better at defending himself, Jacob went to the field often and always showed up early. "Hey, Caldwell! Where are you?" He took a few steps into the woods and called out even louder. "I'm not here to play games!"

He laughed when he heard the leaves rustle. "Your sneak attack isn't working, either. You're making too much noise. Hurry up and get out here. I can't wait any longer for us to fight."

"Me neither." Aldjor said as he stepped out from behind a bush. "Glad to see me?"

As Jacob backed up, four other Haggeldies, each more disgusting than the next, came out of the woods. Circling him, they scraped their bony fingers against his ribs, arms and face. He could taste their foul stench.

"You brought us here to fight this scraggly thing? Couldn't you take care of him yourself?"

"I could, but you didn't want to miss out on the fun, did ya?"

"He's a runt."

"He ain't got no muscles."

"Guys," Aldjor explained, "it'll be a blast. We can do anything we want. He can't stop us."

"Can we jump on him?"

"Can we kick him in the head?"

"I said, 'we can do anything we want.'"

"You're right, Aldjor. This will be fun."

"Maybe if you give up right away, we won't beat on you as much, right guys?" They snorted and howled at the idea that they'd be anything but mean.

"Leave me alone," he said, pretending to be strong, though he couldn't keep his body from shaking.

"Aw, we scared the poor baby."

"What a wiener."

"Lame."

Jacob had learned some about hand-to-hand combat, yet he was far from ready for a real battle with even one Haggeldie, say nothing of five. Plus, he was taking to heart everything they said, despite Caldwell's warning.

Aldjor grabbed his arms and tossed him to the ground. His sword went flying. The others stomped on his chest and legs, making hundreds of cuts all over his body with their hair. They'd drawn first blood.

"Gonna cry?"

"Snowflake."

"Pansy."

"Loser."

He wrapped his head in his arms to protect himself from both their punches and their putdowns. They were having such a good time he wondered if they'd ever stop.

Whoosh! One of the Haggeldies was ripped from his body and sent flying through the air. It picked itself up off the ground, shook its fist in anger, and yelled, "I'll be back for you!" Then it disappeared into the woods. The same thing happened to another Haggeldie. Whoosh! Then another and another. Whoosh, whoosh!

Each time a Haggeldie was tossed aside, it felt like a strong wind had blown over his body. When only Aldjor remained, Jacob looked up to see a pine tree standing over them. It was the Great Pine who had chased him into the basement. *Why was one scary creature who came after him fighting the other scary creatures who came after him?*

Once Aldjor was torn off him and ran away, he carefully stood up and brushed the dirt from his clothes.

"You okay?" the Great Pine asked.

"Uh, yeah, um . . . th-thanks."

"No problem. It looked like you could use some help."

As automatic as breathing, a sarcastic remark shot out of his mouth. "What made you think I needed help, the fact that I was flat on my back with five fat Haggeldies on top of me?"

Oh, crap! He immediately ducked to avoid being swatted by a branch himself.

"Ho, ho, ho. Hilarious. You did look funny lying on your back. Ha, ha, ha." All the Great Pine's branches shook with laughter, causing a large number of needles and pine cones to land on his head.

"What's so funny?"

"You are. But then I've always liked your strange sense of humor, probably because I have one myself."

"You think I have a good sense of humor?"

"I said 'strange.' But yeah, some of the comments you make to your sister on your way to the bus, they really get me going."

"You laugh at me?"

"You're very entertaining."

He got up and brushed more debris out of his hair. "Well, you dump a lot of needles when you're being 'entertained.'"

"It happens. People think it's because the wind is blowing. But usually us trees are just having a good time. There's a lot of fun to be had."

"You weren't laughing when you chased me into the basement. You almost crushed me."

The Great Pine leaned forward. "I was pretty angry, I'll admit."

"Why? I never did anything to you."

"Really? Every time you walk past me, you rip off one of my branches or some of my needles, and throw them on the ground like it's nothing."

"What's the big deal about that?"

"It hurts! My branches and needles are part of me. How would you like it if I peeled a scab off one of your sores or pulled a bunch of hair out of your head every time I saw you?"

"I'd get real tired of it."

"And then there's this." The Great Pine

pointed to holes in his bark. "This is from when you started pounding nails into me."

"I was making a ladder so I could climb you."

"Do you have any idea how much it hurt when you did that?"

"A lot, I suppose."

"Well, it got my sap boiling, so I went after you. I thought if I gave you a good scare, you'd leave me alone. But you didn't stop, so I had to make it worse each time.

"Sorry. Look." Jacob crossed his heart. "I promise to never rip anything off you or pound nails into you ever again, okay?"

"It's a deal. And I promise to never chase you into a basement again."

"Good." Jacob nodded his head. "Hey, how long have you been standing there?"

"Let me see . . .I've been here at the edge of these woods for about thirty years—I guess. The forest is a second home to me."

"No, I mean, how long have you been standing there watching me?"

"Oh, only a few days."

"Kind of sneaky for a tree to hide in the woods, don't you think?"

"I pulled it off, though, didn't I? You never knew I was here." The Great Pine's joke got both of them laughing which caused more needles and pine cones to drop down on Jacob.

"Have you seen me every time I've been in Chimeran?"

"I've seen you . . .every time I've seen you. Can't say when I haven't. It's like Caldwell said, 'You never know who's watching. It could be an enemy, or it could be a friend.'"

"Which one are you?"

"You have to ask?"

Jacob shrugged. "I guess not. It's just . . .it's hard to think of you being on my side—because of all the times you almost killed me. You're not exactly who I thought you were."

"Sometimes we picture someone a certain way for so long we can't see anything else about them. But you can't understand who anyone is if you only look at them from far away. There's more to trees, and people, than you'd guess."

"What people are you talking about?"

"The ones you only think you know. It's important to see them the way they are rather than the way you imagine them to be. You wouldn't want anyone to see you the wrong way, would you?"

"I suppose not." He'd always assumed that whatever people thought about him or said about him was the absolute truth, anyway.

"Can't you give me a hint? Like, who are these people?"

"Okay, here's a clue. 'Every day and every night they're in your life.'"

Jacob threw up his hands. "What does that mean?"

"I can't explain it; otherwise, it's an answer,

not a clue. Besides, this is something everybody has to figure out on their own."

"Well, I have no idea what you're talking about."

"Just pay more attention to the people around you, take the chance of getting to know someone new and remember the clue."

"'Every day and every night they're in my life.' Got it."

The images of the Great Pine, the field and the woods faded as Jacob woke up in his own bed. He immediately went over to the window to check on the tree, which stood in its familiar place.

"Thanks again, friend. I promise to do my best. And I'll remember the clue."

As needles fell to the ground, he was sure the Great Pine approved.

Chapter Eleven – With New Eyes

If Jacob was going to see people differently, as the Great Pine suggested, he'd have to start with one person. But who? He already knew way too much about Tommy. He didn't want to know more about Olivia. And Liz was way too scary. That left Smelly Delly.

To accomplish his goal, he'd work like a private detective. He'd watch Smelly Delly from a distance as he gathered the information he needed. And no one would suspect a thing.

Right away he saw how Del sat by himself on the bus every day. *No friends,* he noted. Then he heard Del laugh along with the kids who made fun of him. *Keeps his head up,* he logged. But the most surprising discovery was that when Del was called a name, he didn't put the other kid down in return. *How does he do that?* Jacob wondered.

At school, he followed Del down the hall, staying a few steps behind him and out of sight. When a couple older boys pushed Del into the lockers, he pretended to search for something in his backpack while keeping one eye on what they did to Del.

"Hey, Smelly, how ya doin today?" one asked as another grabbed the cap off his head for a game of keep away.

"Never saw anything this ugly before."

"It's butt ugly!"

"We should put it on his butt."

"He already does . . .on his butt head."

"His head does look like a butt, doesn't it?"

"Smells like a butt, too, except he needs a butt crack."

One of them put Del in a headlock while the other used a marker to draw a line down the middle of his forehead.

"There's your butt crack, smelly head."

Finally, they threw his cap down and crushed it under their feet as they walked away. Del calmly picked it up, pushed it back into shape and hung it in his locker. Then, he wiped the mark off his forehead before moving on

Wow! He gets pushed around worse at school than on the bus.

In their first hour geography class, Jacob normally spaced out when Ms. Fenzl talked about the Roman ruins or how states got their borders. Today, he watched one of the kids sitting across from Del threaten him. "Hey, Smelly, better not make us look bad just cause you have your homework done."

Still, the next time Ms. Fenzl asked a question, Del raised his hand. *Determined to be himself, no matter what.*

The Great Pine was right. When he looked at Del with new eyes, he saw him in new ways, but he needed to find out more. So, the next Saturday, he rode his bike toward Smelly Delly's place. He'd ridden past it many times on the way to Tommy's, though he'd never paid much attention. Today, he stopped at the end of the driveway to take it all in.

The house had missing shingles and broken windows. The paint on every building was faded or peeling. In the middle of the yard, long grass grew up around a junk car. Rusty scrap metal sat in a pile near the driveway. Closer to the house, long boards and broken branches were thrown together in a heap.

A sagging barn sat across the driveway. So many boards were missing, Jacob could see through it to the field beyond. Next to the barn was a fenced-in area for pigs, though most of the fence was broken or gone. To the left of that stood a chicken coop with a door that hung by one hinge. This meant the chickens roamed through the yard, competing with the pigs to make the most noise and the biggest mess. Everything on the farm looked beaten down.

This place is nasty!

"Well, if it isn't Jacob Tannin. How are you doing today?"

Where'd she come from? He hadn't seen Del's mother. This was bad, real bad. Detectives don't get caught by the people they're following.

"Are you here to see Del?"

"Oh, uh . . .hi, Mrs. Seliger."

"Now, now, you don't have to stand out here. Come on in. I'm sure Del's not too busy to spend time with one of his best friends."

One of his best friends? Where'd she get that idea? She put her arm on his shoulder and nudged him forward. "Del talks about you all the time. Don't worry; it's nothing terrible."

He pushed his bike up the driveway as they walked towards the house. When the pigs and chickens crossed in front of them, Del's mom teased, "Bacon and eggs on the run." Jacob never thought this joke was funny before, still he laughed politely while a hundred questions went through his mind. *What would he say to Del once he got in the house? How long would he have to stay? Would he have to talk to Del on the bus now? Would other kids pick on him if he did? Why hadn't he just ridden past?*

With his first step in the front door, a strong odor hit him in the face. It was the stink Del brought onto the bus, the stink that earned him his nickname. Everyone thought Smelly Delly stunk because he didn't shower. Maybe there was a different explanation.

In the front room, he came face-to-face with a mountain of things: dead plants, books stacked on top of filing cabinets, bags full of plastic bags, bunches of wicker baskets, empty plastic milk jugs, tin cans, toilet paper rolls, glass jars filled with left over bits of soap, games, newspapers, broken toys, purses, For Sale signs, leftover pizza boxes, magazines, a baby carriage, Christmas decorations, partially used candles, and a large bird cage—without the bird.

There were storage boxes, too—dozens of them placed on top of each other with mirrors and picture frames shoved into the spaces in between. Each box was labeled with what was packed inside, things like used light bulbs, silverware, sewing material, CDs, ceramic dishes, calendars, screws and bolts. One was even marked, "pieces of string too short to save."

Piles touched the ceiling in most places. Boxes covered the floor, except for a narrow path through the room. Here was the secret behind Smelly Delly's smell. His mom was a hoarder. The musty odor from all the things she couldn't throw away stuck to him and brought him trouble.

"My mom keeps lots of stuff, doesn't she?" Del called out from the next room. Jacob had been so busy looking around; he never looked up to see where the path would take him.

"Come on in. You may enter my bedroom," Del said with an air of royalty.

His high-sounding welcome didn't match what Jacob saw. Against one wall sat the bed—where he was lying. Next to it was a small table which held Del's math book. On the other side of the bed was a single wooden chair. Stacked everywhere else was more of the stuff his mom was saving. There was almost as much in his room as in the front room.

How did Del live in this mess. How did he get his homework done? How could he eat when everything stunk? And why was he in bed on a sunny Saturday afternoon?

Jacob moved to a small space at the end of the bed and considered what to say. Should he invite Del to go for a bike ride? Or should he do something completely crazy like explain how he was spying on him because a pine tree from another world told him to find out more about the people in his life? Neither seemed like a good option, so he said nothing. It didn't matter.

"Hey, I just did my math homework," Del said. "Did you think it was hard?"

"I haven't looked at it, yet." *Who does homework on Saturday?*

"Are you ever going to sit by Liz again? She really likes you."

"I doubt it."

"I guess you figured out my mom never throws anything away." Now he was on a roll. "We've got more of everything than anybody, but we can never find it when we want it. Hey, did you see my dog, Rusty? He didn't put his mouth around your arm and drag you off, did he? He does it so people will play with him. Oh, oh, oh, did you see the rusty car in the front yard? My dad and I are going to restore it. When I turn sixteen, I'll drive it to school. Hey, I could pick you up. We wouldn't have to ride the bus anymore. Cool, right?"

"Yeah, cool," Jacob muttered.

Del rambled from one subject to the next, barely stopping to take a breath. It was hard to keep up, but it was not dull.

In the same tone of voice as when he told Jacob he owned an old dirt bike, he said, "My mom makes me lay down a couple hours every day because I've got leukemia. She's afraid I'll get too tired."

From that point on, Jacob tuned him out. He was stuck on the thought of Del being sick. *How bad was he? Did the leukemia make him small and weak? What was leukemia, anyway? It would suck to have to lie in bed a couple hours every single day.*

Del's mom poked her head in the room. "You boys hungry? I can make some sandwiches."

"No thanks, Mrs. Seliger. I should get going. My parents will be looking for me." Not true, just the best excuse he could come up with at the time.

With more enthusiasm than Jacob wanted him to have, Del said, "I'll see you Monday!"

"Okay."

Great. Del would talk to him when he got on the bus and other people would find out he'd been at Del's house. They'd think the two of them were friends! Jacob didn't need another reason for people to make fun of him.

Del's mom walked him to the front door and squeezed his arm. "I'm so glad you stopped by. It was really good for him. You're a great friend. I can't understand why none of his other friends have been over."

He took a deep breath, raised his eyebrows and said nothing rather than tell her Del didn't have any friends.

"He'll talk about this for days. I hope we'll see you again soon."

"Sure," he responded, even though he'd do anything to never be in that house again. He jumped on his bike and escaped down the driveway. Once he got some distance from the Seliger farm, Jacob slowed down to consider what he'd learned.

Before today, Del was the weird, smelly kid on his bus. Now Jacob knew something real about him. Still, he'd only gotten some facts about Del. He didn't actually know him—which means he didn't accomplish what he'd set out to do. He dreaded the thought of it, yet if he was going to see Del in a new way, he'd have to take another chance—a really big chance.

Monday morning, he took a deep breath, walked down the center aisle of the bus to where Del was and asked, "Can I sit with you?"

Del immediately slid over.

When Willard saw the two of them together, he yelled, "Hey, all the freaks are in one place!" This got other kids talking. "I'd never sit there." "He's gonna stink."

Jacob turned around to get Tommy's reaction. "What is wrong with you?" he mouthed. Jacob shrugged his shoulders and focused on Del.

"I looked up leukemia. It sounds rough."

"It's not too bad. I take medicine and sometimes I'm tired. I see the doctor a lot. Otherwise, it's all good. Hey," Del asked, "did you ever tell your parents what happened with your science project?

"You mean how it exploded because I used too much wood alcohol, sent chunks of marshmallow creme all over the room, and burned a hole in the lab table? Or how I was sent to the office and then had to clean it up during study hall? Uh, no, I did not tell them."

"It was awesome. Everybody thought so."

The rest of the way, Del talked a mile a minute, giving Jacob no chance to say even one word. There was no need, because Del was funny. By the time they got off the bus, Jacob was glad he sat there.

"See ya later, Del."

"You mean, 'smell you later,' right?"

As they laughed, Jacob realized Del was more okay with himself than anyone he knew.

"Hey, man." Tommy punched Jacob in the shoulder. "What was it like sittin' by Smello Dello?""

"Actually, pretty entertaining."

Tommy zipped open his lunch bag to reveal a giant dill pickle in a plastic bag. "More fun than sliding a juicy pickle down Eric Bantle's shirt?"

"You did that?"

"I would have if you'd sat by me. But no, Eric gets to spend his whole day pickle free. It would've been incredible. People would wonder where the smell came from and only we would know."

"At least you've still got a pickle for lunch."

"I can't eat that after I imagined it touching Eric's sweaty back. One pickle totally wasted."

Jacob laughed. "You're crazy."

"Thanks. Hey, is Del crazy, too?"

"You'd be surprised."

"I suppose he's your new best friend, huh?" Tommy raised one eyebrow.

"Don't be an idiot," Jacob said, "You're still my best friend. But you could say he's one of my friends." He paused to let Tommy absorb this news before telling him what else he had in mind. "So . . .so, I don't think we should call him Smelly Delly anymore."

"Man, you suck the fun out of everything."

"Why don't you sit with us on the way home?"

Tommy put his hand on his head. "You're going to sit with him again? Didn't you hear everybody talking?"

"They were going to talk about me anyway. It's . . .well, why not sit with him? Come on, you'll like him once you hang around with him a while."

"I gotta think about it."

On the bus ride home, Tommy walked up to where Jacob and Del were already sitting, shrugged, and sat down. Again, Del talked about a million things while the two of them laughed. And it was the last time either of them ever called him "smelly."

Chapter Twelve – Ditch Diving and Suckers

As the weeks went on, Tommy, Del and Jacob spent more of their Saturdays together. They'd race their bikes down country roads, leave skid marks in the gravel and coast as far as they could with no hands. But their favorite thing by far was ditch diving.

The point of ditch diving was to build up speed, turn their bikes into the ditch and come out the other side with air underneath them. They'd start on the road and end up in the field or start in the field and try to make it to the road. Sometimes mud or weeds slowed them down. Other times they'd crash. But when it worked, they'd land on both wheels, spin in a circle and watch the gravel fly.

Of the three, Del was best because he didn't care how deep the ditch was or how hard he landed. It didn't bother him to fall on the gravel or wind up in the corn stalks either.

One day, after another round of ditch diving, they headed down a road that held its own kind of danger, for it would take them past the Smith place. There they'd be confronted by Mr. Smith himself. Thin as a scarecrow with tobacco juice dripping off his chin onto his bib overalls, he'd chase after anyone who came near his farm. The mean look on his face and the pitchfork in his hand convinced most people to stay away. It also made sneaking past his house the kind of challenge twelve-year-old boys take.

Quietly the three friends approached the Smith place, yet before they even reached the driveway, he was charging toward them. "I told you before; we don't want you around here!" He ran after them till they were out of sight, threatening them with every step.

"Wow! That was fun, not." Tommy said.

"Let's do it again," Del suggested.

"Why? You like getting yelled at by old creepy guys?" Jacob asked.

"We have to show him we can ride on any road we want."

"He might actually stab you with his pitchfork," Jacob warned. "He's that crazy."

"Let him try."

"Man, if he shoved it in you, you'd have holes in your body," Tommy held his chin in his hand and stared up at the clouds as he imagined what would happen next. "In a couple days, there'd be pus comin' out of them, oozin' down your back." He nodded his head, "That would be cool."

"It would never happen because he would never catch me," Del replied.

"It would still be cool." Tommy said. "You know what else is cool? My brother told me there's a creek behind the barn. We should check it out."

"How are we going to do that? We can't even

ride on the road without him going off on us!" said Jacob.

"My brother said Mr. Smith goes to town every Saturday afternoon. We can see the creek before he gets back."

"Your brother makes stuff up. There's probably nothing back there."

"Him and his friends went there once."

"Even if he did, how does he know Mr. Smith is going to town today?"

"I told you. He always does on Saturday."

"The only way to find out," Del argued, "is to go back there ourselves. Besides, doing it would be like payback for all the times he's yelled at us. Are you going to let him tell you what you can do and where you can go?"

Now Tommy and Del leaned forward on their handlebars and stared Jacob down. "Are we going to do this, or not?" Del asked.

"Or," Tommy added, "are you gonna be a weenie and make up some lame excuse?"

"We better not get caught."

"We can't," Tommy insisted. "Nobody'll be there. It's perfect!"

They returned later that day. And since Mr. Smith did not run out to yell at them, they figured he might have actually gone to town. Just to be sure, Tommy was sent up the driveway. No one showed. So Del and Jacob joined him. Then the three of them pedaled around the side of the barn and down a hill. Thirty yards in, Tommy was beaming.

"See? My brother was right."

They dumped their bikes in the thick grass and ran to the creek's edge. From there, they looked down at the brownest water any of them had ever seen. "That's nasty," Jacob said.

"Who cares?" Del tore off his shirt and shoes and jumped in feet first. When nothing bad happened, the others followed. Soon they were squishing their toes in the mud.

"Hey, something's biting me!" Tommy scrambled back on shore, holding out his arms. "What are these things!?"

"Leeches," Jacob yelled. "They're sucking your blood."

"They're all over me! What do I do, what do I do?!"

In mock horror, Del screamed, "Pull them off before all your blood is gone!"

Tommy picked leeches off his body as fast as he could while Jacob and Del laughed so hard they couldn't climb out of the creek if they'd wanted.

"Oh man, how much blood did they take? We shouldn't have come here."

"They sure love the way you taste," Jacob said.

"Yeah," Del added, "They're hungry for you."

"He looks a little pale, doesn't he, Del? What should we do with him after they've drained all the blood out of him?"

"We'll leave his cold, lifeless body on the shore for Mr. Smith."

"No! You can't. We're supposed to watch out for each other, man."

"Jeez," Jacob said, "for somebody who thought pus coming out of Del's body would be cool, you sure are a weenie."

He and Del climbed out of the water and calmly pulled a few leeches off their arms. Then the three of them walked along the edge of the creek till they came to a spot where the water got clearer and shallower. And in those shallow places were some good-sized fish.

"What kind of fish are those?" Jacob pointed at the fattest one.

"Suckers—they're all suckers," Tommy answered.

Del grabbed him. "Suckers? Oh no, they'll drink all our blood! Hold me, Tommy, I'm scared."

"Knock it off!"

"Do you think we could catch them?" Jacob asked.

"My dad used to go spearfishing for suckers," Del said. "We've still got a couple spears in the barn. Let's get 'em."

"All right! Let's spear some fish!" Tommy was back to his old self.

They quickly returned and with spears in hand stalked the shoreline.

"Do we throw 'em at the fish, or what?" Jacob asked.

"Duh! Of course you throw the spear at the fish." Tommy said.

Del didn't waste time talking. He tossed his spear at the first fish he saw. Unfortunately, the fish also saw him and safely swam away. The others cheered his effort anyway.

They'd never done this before, so most of the fish got away, though they eventually caught a half dozen suckers.

"We can take these home," Tommy suggested.

"We'll be like pioneers who went into the wilderness to get food for their families," Jacob supposed. The three looked up at the clouds, imagining their families gathered around a table for a great feast.

"What you boys doin?" Mr. Smith stood close behind them with his arms folded across his chest and a scowl on his face.

"Uh, nothing," they said in unison, turning his way while tossing their spears in the grass behind them.

"It don't look like nothin'!" He spat tobacco juice at their feet. "It looks like you caught some of my fish. You boys had better get out of here and don't ever think about comin' onto my land or fishin' in my creek again, or your parents will hear about it."

They grabbed the spears and their bikes and sped away, only stopping when it was safe.

"We're such suckers," Del declared.

"What do you mean? We're lucky to get away

with our lives." Jacob said.

"We shouldn't have left the fish there. We caught them. They belong to us!"

"The fish were in the creek on his property." Tommy reminded Del.

"It doesn't mean he owns them. Besides, we did all the work. They're ours. Let's go get them."

Jacob had never seen Del so worked up. "But he's watching for us."

"Well," Del took a moment to consider his plan, "we'll do what magicians do. We'll make him look at one thing while we're doing something else." The devious look on Del's face was new.

"Or, we could just go home," Jacob offered.

"No. We have to do it." After he explained what he had in mind, Jacob and Tommy agreed to go along with it, not because they thought it would work, but because if anyone got into trouble, it would be Del, not them.

Part one of the plan had Jacob and Tommy ride up the driveway. Almost instantly, Mr. Smith blocked their way.

"I thought I made it clear I don't want you boys around here."

"We wanted to say we're sorry," Jacob explained.

Mr. Smith jammed his pitchfork into the ground and gave them a hard stare. "All right, what have you got to say for yourselves?"

They took turns telling how at first they only wanted to check out the creek but got carried away because they saw the fish. When Tommy threw in the whole story of how he freaked out over the leeches, even showing off the marks on his arms, Jacob spotted a twinkle in Mr. Smith's eyes.

While they kept him busy with their fake apology, Del implemented part two of his plan. He snuck around the barn and grabbed the three largest fish off the ground. But instead of slipping back out the way he went in, he headed straight toward them!

What's he doing? Jacob wondered.

Going full speed, Del rode right between them and Mr. Smith. Then he cruised into the ditch, caught air and skidded onto the road. Finally, he held up one of the fish and yelled, "Sucker!"

"Come back here with those fish," Mr. Smith yelled as he grabbed his pitchfork and gave chase.

Meanwhile, Jacob heard someone else yelling, "Don't go," the voice called. "Please, don't leave me!" He turned toward the house where he saw a white-haired woman sitting in a wheelchair on the front porch. She had a cast on her arm and a quilt around her shoulders. He wasn't sure who she was, but apparently she thought Mr. Smith was leaving for good.

Tommy punched Jacob in the shoulder. "Come on, man. This is our chance to get out of here." As they rode away, Jacob called out to the woman, "Sorry!"

When they caught up with Del, he was super pumped. "We did it! We got back at old man Smith! And we each get one of these as a reward," he said as he held out a fish. Jacob took his and faked a smile. But after the others rode away, he tossed it in the ditch. It was simpler to throw it out than explain to his parents how he'd gotten it.

At supper, his dad asked, "What were you up to today?"

"Hung out with Tommy and Del."

"Did you do anything interesting?"

"We went past the Smith place."

His dad chuckled. "I suppose he yelled at you."

"Why is he so mean?"

"He's not mean; he's just worried about his mother."

"The woman in the wheelchair?"

"Yup. She gets all worked up over any noise or excitement, so he tries to keep people away."

"He doesn't have to holler at everybody."

"Hollering and running after people with a pitch fork—that's a little out there, I'll admit. But he'd never hurt anyone."

"Will you watch over me that closely if I ever get like her?" his mother teased.

"I don't even own a pitchfork, Mom."

As he pushed the food around his plate, he began to see Mr. Smith in a new light. Sure, he was weird, but who wouldn't try to protect his mother?

That night in Chimeran, Jacob stood in the center of the field as a long line of Haggeldies moved past him, patting him on the back.

"Way to go!"

"You really showed that guy."

"He had it coming."

"Keep up the good work!"

The more they praised him, the more his stomach hurt. Now he understood what was bothering him. He had acted like a Haggeldie!

After the parade of Haggeldies ended, he slumped down next to the rock. Without warning, a wet nose pushed itself against his cheek. Dog slobber! The golden retriever from the farm put his head in Jacob's lap. "I'm going to call you Red." He rubbed Red's ears and explained how the practical joke went wrong.

"I see you found the dog." It was the Man in the Middle. "Or he found you."

"Yeah."

"They're pretty good listeners. Great friends, too—and since you're hiding behind a rock with a sour look on your face, I assume you could use one. What's wrong?"

Jacob stroked Red's neck as he told the whole story one more time. "She seemed so scared. Did she really think he would leave her?"

"At that moment, she did. She's afraid of all sorts of things including unexpected noises and people coming near their house. Why were you there?"

"We were trying to get back at Mr. Smith for hollering at us."

"Did you ever consider there might be more going on with him than you know about?"

Jacob shook his head. "No."

"Mr. Smith's life isn't easy what with taking care of his mother and running the farm."

"You seem to know everything about everybody."

"Let's not get into that right now. Instead, answer one question for me." The Man in the Middle leaned forward. "What's the real reason you feel guilty?"

"I scared his mother?"

"I think you feel guilty because you had already decided Mr. Smith was bad, but when you saw her, you knew you had it wrong."

"I thought he was a Haggeldie." Jacob buried his face even deeper into Red's neck.

"Calling some people good and others bad . . .it's never that simple. By the way, you're not the only one who's upset. Del threw his fish away, too."

"But it was his idea."

"He wanted to find out what it would be like to get back at someone who picked on people. Revenge wasn't as much fun as he thought it would be. One more question. Did you think you were being brave when you tricked Mr. Smith?"

"Yeah. I thought I was standing up for myself."

"You don't feel brave now, though, do you?"

"No."

"When you only think you're brave, you're probably not. And when you've been brave, you won't feel like you do now. Remember that, because soon, you will need to be brave."

Jacob asked, "When will I need to be brave?" But The Man in the Middle was already gone. Red licked his face one more time before bouncing off to chase a butterfly. Meanwhile, he was left to wonder, *What's coming now?*

Chapter Thirteen – Little People in My Lap

"**Y**ou should have seen him, man." Tommy leaned into the bus's aisle to brag. "He was nasty. There was tobacco drool all over his face. He was missing half his teeth. And the ones that weren't missing were like little black beans."

"Weren't you afraid?" one of the kids asked.

"A lot of people would've been cause he's a scary lookin' dude, and mean, too. But it didn't stop me from goin' right up to him and tellin' him what I thought. That's when Del got the fish back."

"Were you there?" one of them asked Jacob.

"Uh, I didn't do much of anything," Jacob mumbled.

"That's right; it was all me," Tommy boasted. "Now, let me tell you how I caught those fish old man Smith wanted to take from us."

While Tommy went on with his stories, Jacob stared out the window. He was quiet the next few times he was in Chimeran, too. Yet Andrea and Caldwell didn't seem to notice, which was good enough for him.

One night, not long after the incident with Mr. Smith, Jacob sat in the cave waiting for his friends. He held his head in his hands and stared at the fire. *Was there a way to make up for what he'd done? Would he ever figure out how to truly*

be brave? What would his next challenge be:
another battle with Haggeldies or something
worse? All the questions made his head hurt.

Then, unexpected and unannounced, she
walked in. Dressed in a dazzling white gown, she
wore white shoes topped off by large white
buttons. The long sleeves on her white gloves
went past her elbows, and a stunning white
jacket covered her shoulders. Sparkling jewels
hung from the edge of a white hat that was
perched on her head, while a white feather lay
along its brim. The light from the fire, reflecting
off her brilliant outfit, made the cave's walls glow.

"Aunt Polly? Is it really you?"

"Jacob, how wonderful to see you! Come
here." With a lavish smile, she pulled him close
for a good long hug. "You're still my favorite
nephew!"

She said this to him every time she saw him,
thinking it was a great joke, since he was her only
nephew. Then she let loose with an enormously
rich laugh—one which never failed to make him
feel better. He was glad to hear both her laughter
and the joke since she hadn't spoken these words
in quite a while.

Aunt Polly Morgan was his mother's aunt.
When Jacob was younger, he'd spend one week
every summer at her house. She didn't have any
children, so she spoiled him. She'd take him to
movies, water parks and malls, treating him to
anything he wanted. It was the most exciting

week of the year.

But then, it was always exciting to be around Aunt Polly because she loved a good time and often did things that were off the wall. Like when she came back from a winter in Florida. She gave everyone "real Florida oranges" to show that she was thinking about them while she was away. When they found out she actually bought those oranges in a grocery store down the street, Aunt Polly just made fun of herself. Everyone else had a good laugh, too. It was typical Aunt Polly.

Her presence reminded him of all the times he felt better than he did at this moment, although he was amazed to see her in Chimeran and surprised she knew who he was. For ever since her stroke, Aunt Polly didn't recognize people she'd been around her whole life. Plus, she talked about attending fancy balls at an extravagant mansion even though everyone knew she hadn't been out of her wheelchair for years, much less out of the nursing home.

And every once in a while, in the middle of one of her fanciful tales, she'd shake her finger at the ground to scold the "little people," who were supposedly standing near the feet of her visitors. As she firmly ordered those "little people" to behave, everyone else in the room would glance at each other out of the corner of their eyes, silently agreeing that she'd lost touch with reality. Here, in Chimeran, though, she was herself again—full of energy and laughing with every word she spoke.

"I can't believe you're here!" Jacob smiled. "And you're dressed so fancy. You . . . you look different from how you are in the nursing home." His face turned red as soon as the words came out. "Sorry, I shouldn't have said anything."

"It's okay, honey. I know I'm in a nursing home and I'm not completely myself there. But here, I am."

He leaned his head into her shoulder. "I . . .I'm glad you're here."

"Are you okay?"

Jacob explained his struggle to be brave along with all his questions. He also admitted how he felt about what he'd done to Mr. Smith.

Aunt Polly listened carefully, as always. "It'll be all right, Jacob. You'll see. You always worry about too many things. Come along with me. I've got to check on those Little People."

As she led him out of the cave and into the woods, he thought, *She says things are going to be all right, but she's still seeing little people.*

Aunt Polly led him farther into the woods than he'd ever gone. And while she walked with confidence along a well-worn path, he constantly checked behind every tree and bush for any Haggeldie who might leap out at them.

"Aaah!" He jumped as a black bird flew up in front of him.

"Is there something going on with you?" she asked. "You're awfully jittery."

"No, no, ah, a bird surprised me, that's all."

"Well, we better keep moving. We don't want to miss the party."

From that point on, he made sure to be no more than one step behind her.

In the end, the path opened up onto a beautifully landscaped yard which was larger than the field where he'd spent most of his time in Chimeran. It was filled with bushes trimmed to look like apes, rhinos, leopards, crocodiles, pterodactyls, polar bears, giraffes and all sorts of other animals.

In the center of the yard, a monstrous stone mansion stood forty stories high. It had hundreds and hundreds of windows spread across the front, marking hundreds and hundreds of rooms inside the mansion itself. At least ten large pillars held up a roof which covered the grand entrance.

"Isn't it something? I come here as often as I can. There are always dinners or dances. It's one party after another."

"Whose mansion is it?"

"Why, it belongs to the Man in the Middle."

Jacob was in awe. Not only because the mansion was fantastic, but also because it was real. She wasn't making this up, at least.

"Is that why you're wearing so much white? Is there another dance?"

"Why else would I dress so stylishly, young man? There happens to be a birthday party here today. Now, where are those Little People? I can't leave them alone for long, otherwise they get in trouble."

"Wait a minute. Aunt Polly, what little people are you talking about?"

"The ones I always scold. I've told you about them many times. Haven't you been paying attention?"

"They're real?"

She let out another of her generous laughs. "Oh, Jacob, of course they're real! What did you think—I'd lost my mind completely?"

"Well. . . um. . .ah. . .we all thought you were seeing things. Mom said your medication might be causing it. Don't you think it's a little odd for someone to be in the middle of a sentence then, all of a sudden, start yelling at little people no one else sees?"

"Jacob Tannin, you listen to me." She wagged her finger at him a bit. "Those Little People are as real as you and me and the mansion right in front of you. I am not crazy. Come along. I'll show you."

They took a stone pathway to the back gardens, which filled several more acres. "First, you better explore things for a while," she said.

He rushed off to splash in the seven fountains and took in the smells from hundreds of thousands of flowers. He watched fish swim in the ponds and climbed trees in the orchard.

As he sat on a thick branch, eating the apple he'd chosen for a snack, he laughed out loud, not only because he was having fun, but also because he was seeing the obvious. Aunt Polly was more than he imagined her to be.

When he did laugh, laughter came back at him. It wasn't the deep, rich laugh of his aunt, though. It was more like a child's giggle.

"Aunt Polly," he called down to her, "Why does my laugh echo off the mansion but my voice doesn't? Listen."

First he yelled, "Awoo, Awoo." There was no echo. Next he gave a loud laugh, and laughter came back at him. "See what I mean?"

"That's not an echo, dear. Do it again."

He let out the best fake laugh he could and got the same response.

"If it's not an echo, what is it?"

"Well, let's make a game of it. We'll see if you can figure it out." Aunt Polly let loose with a thunderous laugh, to which there were several giggles in response.

"Where is that coming from?"

"I'll give you a hint. Look at the bush in the corner, the one with blue flowers. See if you notice anything different about it when I laugh."

When she laughed, Jacob not only heard giggles, he also saw several small mouths open up near the blue flowers. It was like someone saying "aah" for the dentist.

"Do it again, Aunt Polly."

Again she laughed and again a few small mouths popped open.

"Was that somebody's mouth?"

"It sure was."

"Who's?"

"The Little People you say don't exist."

"But I didn't see a whole person, just mouths."

"Exactly. You can't see them because they blend into the background, like chameleons. They hide to protect themselves. Plus, they're kind of shy. But when they talk or laugh, you can see their mouths."

He stared at the bush with all his might. "Is there a way to see more than just their mouths?"

"Of course there is. But you have to get them to trust you. They'll only let you see them if they feel safe around you. I see them all the time."

"So, in the nursing home, when you look at my legs and tell the Little People to behave. . ."

"They're right at your feet, making faces and sticking out their tongues. They like to make fun of people who can't see them."

"That's the way they are, huh?"

With this new information, he climbed down and sat in front of the bush. "I can't see you, but you're in there. You heard her tell me. Look, you can trust me. I'm her favorite nephew. I wouldn't hurt you any more than she would. Besides, we're a lot alike. I've always been smaller than everyone else, and I like to make fun of people, too."

He stuck out his tongue, made a weird face and laughed. He could see the mouths of several Little People who laughed back at him. Since they seemed to enjoy what he'd done, he did it several more times. Before long, like children moving out from behind their mother's skirt, six Little People emerged from the bush.

Each was only a foot tall and would easily fit inside his backpack. Like two-year-old children, they had chubby cheeks and sweet smiles, although he later learned they were as old as the oldest trees in the forest. Their faces were purple with a hint of blue around the eyes, while their bodies were gray. Their wings were like purple cellophane, faint enough to see through. They had brown tails which ended with a furry black tip, shaped like an arrow. And although they could fly, they also had arms and legs much like his.

As Jacob continued to make goofy faces, the Little People crept closer till all six of them launched themselves toward him. They jumped on him, tickled him and played on his lap. It was like being overrun by puppies. Jacob laughed till his stomach hurt.

"That's enough! I think he realizes you like him," Aunt Polly gently scolded them.

The Little People climbed out of his lap and stood in front of him like children who got caught doing something they clearly enjoyed.

Then Aunt Polly called out across the whole back garden. "What about the rest of you?" One after the other, Little People popped out from every imaginable hiding place—some stood on the grass while others hovered in midair.

"Wow! There are dozens and dozens of you guys!"

Soon, they charged at him as well. But before they reached him, he ran away. "You'll never get me!" His dare turned into an old-fashioned game of catch and chase, which went on and on until they all collapsed in the middle of the yard. Jacob hadn't been this happy or laughed this hard in forever.

As they lay there, the Little People inched closer and closer till they were snuggling together in one big pile. One by one, Jacob and his new friends closed their eyes.

When he was almost asleep, Aunt Polly leaned over to whisper, "I'm going to the party now, so you rest. And know that you are perfect in every way." *Perfect in every way?* That wasn't true about anyone, and especially not him. Still, he was too tired to argue.

Before long, he woke up in his own bed. Aunt Polly, the Little People, and the mansion were gone, but the words stayed with him. So did the question, *Why would anybody say that about me?*

Chapter Fourteen – Visiting Aunt Polly

Once a month, the Tannin family made the thirty-mile trip to Eureka to visit Great-aunt Polly at the nursing home. Ever since her stroke, she couldn't walk and didn't remember much. The first time she didn't recognize Jacob, he was extremely disappointed. "She's still there," his mother explained, "inside—and you can hold onto the memories you made together for both of you."

Their latest trip came one day after Aunt Polly's eightieth birthday. It was also one day after Jacob had seen her in Chimeran. He was excited to ask her about the Little People and the Man in the Middle, if she remembered anything at all.

They found her sitting near a large window watching hummingbirds flutter back and forth to a feeder. Jacob's mom was the first to give her a hug. "Aunt Polly, how great to see you. It's Marie, remember?" His mom was always hopeful they'd catch Aunt Polly on a good day.

"Have I met you folks before?" she asked.

"You have, many times," Jacob's mom explained. "Remember Harold, my husband, and our children, Olivia and Jacob? We're all here to celebrate your birthday."

As introductions were made, Aunt Polly looked each one over as if meeting them for the first time. Jacob watched for any sign she might remember seeing him in Chimeran but there was none.

"It's nice of you folks to come and see me. Why don't you sit down so we can visit? You can tell me all about yourself."

Without hesitation, Jacob's mom took control of the conversation, sharing all the latest news about the family. "Cousin Betty got a job at the post office. We were so happy for her, what with all the bills piling up from her husband's surgery. We did tell you about it, right? Something went wrong when James had his gall bladder out. Poor man, he spent a whole month in the hospital. Oh, I haven't told you the best news of all. Elvira had a baby girl the other day. We were hoping she'd hold out until your birthday, but you can't tell a child what day to be born on, can you?"

"My birthday? Is today my birthday?"

"No, yesterday was your birthday. But we're going to celebrate it with you today. We brought a cake, some party hats, even a present."

Aunt Polly spied the box in Jacob's hands. "What is it?"

"How about if you open it and find out?"

Marie handed the box to Aunt Polly who held it on her lap for a long while, as if it were a treasure too valuable to be revealed in a rush. Finally, she took a deep breath and undid one piece of tape, then the next and the next, making sure not to tear any of the wrapping paper. Her eyes sparkled when she pulled a brightly colored shawl from the box.

"We thought you could wear it whenever you feel a chill."

"Oh, thank you, thank you. It's lovely!" But instead of wrapping the shawl around her, she folded it up and put it back in the box. "Would you please set this down for me?" she asked, holding it out to Jacob.

He placed the present on the small table between him and Olivia. For the next few minutes, Marie talked about the farm, the weather, and anything else she could think to talk about until Aunt Polly spotted the box again.

"What's in the box?"

"Your birthday present."

"For me? I can't wait to see what it is."

"Do you want to open it?"

"Oh, that would be wonderful."

"Jacob, give Aunt Polly her present, would you?"

Everyone played along as she went through the whole process of taking the shawl out, saying "Thank you, it's lovely," folding it up, putting it back in the box and handing it to Jacob.

A few minutes later, it happened again.

"What's in the box?"

"Your birthday present."

"For me? What is it? Can I open it?"

"Why not?" Jacob mouthed to Olivia. "It's not like she's seen it before."

The two of them giggled as Aunt Polly carefully examined the shawl once again. She was just as excited about it this time as she had been the first time she'd seen it. From then on, right up through the seventh and final time she inspected her present, Jacob and Olivia had to cover their mouths in order to control their laughter.

But Aunt Polly didn't care. She just thought they were happy for her. And she was definitely happy, for as far as she was concerned, every few minutes she got another birthday present.

Announcing, "It's time for cake!" Marie put an end to the whole "birthday present" adventure. Eighty candles were lit, everyone sang, "Happy birthday" and after scraping wax off the icing, the cake was cut.

The huge smile on Aunt Polly's face told them she enjoyed every second of her party. "It was such fun to have you all sing to me, especially the Little People. They have awfully good voices."

It was the first time she'd mentioned them since Chimeran. Jacob looked near everyone's feet, hoping to spot one with their mouth open. Yet there was no sign of them.

"Young man, the Little People aren't by your feet. They're sitting right here—next to me. After all, I am the birthday girl!" She nodded approvingly at her invisible guests.

"We're not going to have to share any cake with those little people, are we?" Marie joked, trying to move past the subject.

"No, they don't like sweets. And even if they did, they wouldn't eat much."

Jacob smiled at his great-aunt's insistence that the Little People were real despite all the others who thought she was hallucinating. Only he knew she was telling the truth, although he still couldn't see them and definitely couldn't say anything.

"I'm afraid we have to go," Marie said. They took Aunt Polly back to her room where she opened her present one more time while Jacob and Olivia grinned. Then, they took turns giving hugs.

"I love you," Marie said. "We'll see you in a little while, okay?" Harold and Olivia went next.

As Jacob reached down to say goodbye to his Aunt Polly, she pulled him close. "Remember, you're perfect in every way."

He quickly pulled back and looked in her eyes. The expression on her face was no different than it had been all day. Yet, her words had been very clear. Maybe it was just a coincidence that she'd said the same thing as the night before.

On the drive home, Jacob wondered what those words meant and why she said it to him. After all, no one was perfect. The only way her words made sense was if he thought of them as a challenge to become a better person.

Okay, he resolved. *I'll try to do everything I can to deserve someone saying I'm perfect in every way!* Unfortunately, this way of thinking only made it harder for him to discover the real meaning behind her words.

Chapter Fifteen – Hidden Haggeldies

Determined to be a better person, Jacob did his homework each night, cleaned his room without being told and put extra effort into his training in Chimeran. He'd get to the field early and warm up by pretending to fight a tree, though he never actually touched any tree so he could keep his promise to the Great Pine.

"Ha! Take that. You're no match for the famous swordsman, Jacob Tannin. Pull back your branches! Grow thicker bark! Nothing you do matters because I am your master. You will obey my command or pay the price!"

"Aaarrgh." Instantly, chills shot up his spine. He backed into an open space and spun around to check for Haggeldies.

"Aaarrgh."

"Where are you hiding, Aldjor?"

"Well, well, if it isn't the 'famous' swordsman, Jacob Tannin," Aldjor said as he stepped out from behind a large bush.

"You better stay away."

"Or what?"

"Hey, Aldjor, is he gonna try to hurt all of us or just you?"

Jacob turned around to see the same four Haggeldies who'd beaten him down the last time.

"He thinks he's better than he was before."

Aldjor explained.

"He looks like the same loser to me," a second Haggeldie said.

"What do you think you can do to us anyway? Should we be scared?" Aldjor asked. They laughed at the thought of it.

While Jacob wasn't happy to see them, a part of him had been waiting for a second chance to prove himself. Before they could surround him, he moved to his left and onto higher ground. Already he was doing better than before. Looking down from his perch, he held up his sword. "You want to fight? Come on. We'll fight."

"How stupid are you?" Aldjor asked. "You aren't ready for us just because you've been playing games with your little friends. You'll never be better than us. And this time the tree isn't here to save you!"

He glanced over to where the Great Pine usually stood. It was gone. The Haggeldies rushed him, but he held his ground. Then he attacked one at a time, as Caldwell had taught him. He focused on Aldjor, thinking that if he got rid of the leader, the rest would give up.

While this battle went on longer than the last one, the outcome was the same. They knocked the sword from his hand, pushed his face into the dirt and took turns kicking him.

Curled up in a ball, he tried to block their blows with his arms. "Don't do that!"

"Poor little fellow wants us to stop."

"Sounds like he's giving up."

One of them leaned over and yelled. "Say it! Say, 'I give up.'"

"Okay, I give up."

"Say it louder."

"I give up! You win." Jacob shouted.

"I knew it."

"He's pathetic."

After a few more blows, Aldjor declared, "You belong to us, now. We can take you down any time we want." At this last insult, they all snickered and went back into the woods while Jacob laid there, too afraid to move.

"You need to get up." It was the Man in the Middle. "If you stay where you are, you'll only feel more helpless."

Jacob's body shook as he forced himself to stand. "I did everything wrong."

"You're not the first one to lose a battle or to get upset about it."

"Nobody loses as much as I do."

"That's not true. Everybody is defeated at some time. But people who are brave keep going. They also do something you hardly ever do."

"What's that?"

"They give themselves a break."

"It's not my fault those stinkin' Haggeldies came after me. I hate them!" He grabbed a chunk of sod and threw it as far as he could.

"Hate's a powerful emotion, Jacob. It can take over." As he spoke, the circle of mirrors rose up around them a second time. Jacob didn't want to look at himself, yet there he was—covered with sweat and dirt—pathetic, just like the Haggeldies said.

"Look closely. Do you see any changes?"

"Mud's stuck to my body. I've got bruises on my face. There's a rip in my shirt up by my shoulder. I. . .I. . .oh, no!"

Coming through the hole in his shirt was a lump of fat, and growing out of it, was a small patch of hair. Jacob tried to push the lump back into his body. "Are they contagious? Did I get this from them?"

"In a way. It comes from anger and hatred like theirs."

The Man in the Middle put his hands on Jacob's shoulders and looked him squarely in the eyes. "If you give up on yourself and give in to this hatred you feel, you'll change."

"I'll become one of them?"

"You will if you don't let go of your anger."

Jacob thought about what the Haggeldies had done to him and realized he didn't just hate them, he enjoyed hating them.

"I'm not coming to Chimeran anymore, then. That way I won't have to deal with Haggeldies."

The Man in the Middle chuckled. "Haggeldies are everywhere. You may not spot them as easily in Telluris because they look like you. But on the inside, they're the same as they are in Chimeran."

"Haggeldies are hiding in my everyday life?

Great."

"And the possibility of acting like a Haggeldie is hiding in everyone—even in you. After all, don't you complain, don't you make fun of others in order to feel better about yourself? And didn't you just say you hated Haggeldies?"

"So my battle with Haggeldies will never end because they're everywhere? Thanks for the good news!"

"You're better off knowing the truth."

"And the best advice you have for me after I just gave up in my battle with Haggeldies—is 'Don't give up'? There should be something more than that."

"There is, but you're not ready for it. Be patient. Everything and everyone are not what they appear to be. Neither are you. Look in the mirrors again."

The hairy lump of fat on his shoulder had shrunk.

"It'll be gone soon because you're not as angry as you were a few minutes ago."

The mirrors slid back into the ground and the Man in the Middle walked away as Andrea and Caldwell came up to him.

"Whoa, what happened to you?" Caldwell asked. "You look awful."

"Haggeldies happened to me."

There'd be no training that day. Instead, Jacob told about his fight and shared the warnings the Man in the Middle had given. In the end, they took an oath to watch over each other so none of them would ever turn into a Haggeldie.

Chapter Sixteen – Looking for a Better Way

"**G**o deep!"

"I am."

"No, deeper."

Jacob threw the ball as far as he could while also doing the play-by-play. "Quarterback Jacob Tannin goes back in the pocket. He escapes the rush before unleashing a Hail Mary into the end zone. The ball is tipped by the free safety. Ooooh—the wide receiver, Tommy Leaver, comes out of nowhere to catch the ball for a touchdown as time runs out! The crowd goes wild. Tommy Leaver will be MVP of this year's championship game."

Tommy wiggled his hips and spiked the ball. "All right! I'm the MVP and I am going to Disneyworld!"

"All wrong," Willard said as he picked up the football. "You're the d-o-p-e. And you are goin' nowhere!"

"Come on, man, give me the ball."

"You want it, take it."

Tommy reached for the football, but with Willard's hand on his forehead, he wasn't getting anywhere close.

"The ball belongs to me. Give it back!"

Willard tapped Tommy on the head with it. "I don't feel like it."

Without thinking, Jacob ran full speed at the two of them and launched himself into Willard's side. They hit the ground together while Tommy's football came free.

"You don't get to take our football."

Jacob had spoken up for himself, but his words had no impact on Willard, who grabbed him by the shoulders, rolled him onto his back and sat on his stomach.

"Are you always this stupid or is today special? I'm taking the football and giving you a purple nurple, lamo," Willard laughed, then pinched Jacob's nipples.

"Oww."

Within seconds one of the teachers on lunch duty separated them. "Enough!" Within minutes, they were both staring at the principal's desk.

"Anybody want to tell me what happened?"

Willard looked up, his eyes as big as the moon. "They were throwin' the football around, and I tried to catch one of the passes, to be part of the game. I guess he didn't like it, so he jumped me."

"You're lying! You took our ball and wouldn't give it back!"

"Jacob, calm down. There's no reason to be so angry. Did you have something else you wanted to say, Willard?"

"Just that I don't get why he was so freaked out. I was only trying to have some fun."

"No, you weren't!"

"What did I say about holding your temper, Jacob?"

"But he always does this. He calls us names, hits us and knocks our stuff around."

"Is there any truth to what he's saying, Willard?"

"Look, I didn't do nuthin', honest. Just 'cause I'm big, people make me out to be a bully. Well, I got feelings, too." He crossed his arms, a forlorn look on his face.

"Jacob, is it possible you misunderstood Willard's intentions? Maybe he did want to play catch with you but was unsure how to ask?"

Jacob slumped in his chair. The argument couldn't be won. And he'd be the one in trouble if he didn't play along.

"Jacob?"

"Yes, sir."

"Did you have to knock Willard to the ground to get the football?"

"No."

"I thought not. Boys, here at Lakeside, we don't think highly of students who get into fights. It shows a great disrespect for each other and for the whole school. We want you to have good memories of this place after you move on to high school. You won't, though, unless you find a way to get along with each other. Do you boys think you can do that?"

"Sure can, Mr. Naples."

Jacob, how about you?"

"I guess."

"You can do better than 'I guess,' can't you?"

"Yes, sir."

The principal sighed. "It seems like every time I give you kids an inch, you take a mile." He paused long enough to make Jacob wonder what he would say next. "But I'll give you a second chance, this time. Neither of you will get detention. I will contact your parents, though, to tell them what happened here today." The principal paused. "One last thing, before you go back to the classroom, I want you to shake hands to show that all this is behind us."

Willard stuck his hand out right away while Jacob slowly reached out and grabbed it. Of course, the smiling principal didn't notice how tightly Willard squeezed Jacob's fingers.

"That's more like it. Now get back to learning. And I don't want to have any more trouble from either of you. Got it?"

As soon as they hit the hallway, Willard let out a huge laugh. "You got in trouble, short and stupid."

"You did, too."

"Big deal. My parents won't care. But what do ya think your parents will say when the principal tells them you were in a fight?"

He was right. His parents would be upset. So as soon as he got home, Jacob confessed to everything, except the part about Willard always messing with him.

"I get it. Boys get in fights sometimes," his dad said. "I did when I was your age. Still, there's always a better way to deal with people who make you angry. Don't you think?"

"Yeah." He said it to stay out of trouble, yet if there was a better way to deal with Willard, he had no idea what it was.

Chapter Seventeen – Into the Tunnel

"You're doing way better." It was the first compliment Andrea had ever given him.

"Thanks," he responded as he swung his sword across her body.

"You still won't get me, though."

Since his latest loss to the Haggeldies, Jacob's goal was to become the master sword fighter he had claimed to be. And Andrea was good enough to turn him into one. Today, the training went on so long, they could barely lift their arms at the end of it.

"Caldwell took you into the cave, right?"

"Yeah."

"What did you think?"

"Just a lot of rocks. Kind of boring."

"Did you look behind the rocks?"

"No."

"Then you haven't seen anything. Come with me." She dragged him down the steps and straight to the back of the cave.

"Still think it's boring?"

In front of him were seven entrances to seven tunnels. He ran from one to the next and back again, looking into each. All he could see was darkness.

"Where do these go?"

"Lots of places, I guess. I've never been in any

of them." A smile came over her face. "Want to try one?"

"Sure, but which one?"

"I don't care. You choose."

He looked them over carefully, taking into account the shape of the entrance and the size of the echo which came back at him when he screamed into it. Finally, he settled on the center tunnel. "I've got a good feeling about this one."

As soon as he made his choice, Andrea pushed past him, "Come on then—hurry up."

The first part of the tunnel was a rock path with rock walls, which were cold and wet to the touch. It was mostly dark, so they kept their hands on one wall as they made their way. About ten minutes in, they saw lights shimmering in the distance.

"You think the tunnel leads back into the woods?" Jacob asked. "That could be the sun shining."

"It's got to be something way better than that."

They hurried on to where the tunnel opened up into an area twice the size of the main room of the cave. And everywhere there was glass. There were clear glass stems rising out of the stone floors. On top of the stems bloomed blue, gold, red, yellow, purple and green crystal flowers. There were glass shrubs with glass berries on them and glass fruit trees with glass fruit hanging from each branch.

"What is this place?" Jacob asked.

"It looks like a garden—a glass garden." Andrea rubbed one of the petals with her fingertips. "Everything is so smooth. I wonder if it's alive."

Throughout the garden, they found glass figurines on top of glass pedestals and glass fountains where they could splash in the clearest water. Above them, the sunlight poured in through glass openings shaped like eyeballs and made everything sparkle.

Jacob shielded his eyes. "Everything's so bright. I should have brought sunglasses."

"Yeah, but this is still the most beautiful place ever."

He nodded in agreement. Everything was spectacular. And the colors were intense. Some of the glass even acted like mirrors in a fun house. While they raced from one flower or figurine to the next to laugh at the strange reflections they made, noises from the next part of the tunnel began to invade the space. At first, it sounded like gentle thunder in the distant sky. But as the volume rose, it became wilder, like a pack of snarling dogs. Jacob tried to ignore the uproar, yet neither of them could pretend they didn't hear it.

"Man, that's annoying," he said. "What is it?"

"There's only one way to find out."

"You mean leave the garden?"

"It's an adventure. And we'll end up with a

great story to tell Caldwell."

Not the kind to shy away from the unknown, Andrea quickly headed into the next section of the tunnel. Jacob stumbled after her with eyes wide open.

The first part of this tunnel was the same as the one they'd come out of except the light from the glass garden shone behind them, allowing them to see where they were going. Once they turned a corner, though, it was as if a door had slammed shut. They couldn't even see each other. So, they moved slowly and held hands to make sure they stayed together. Eventually, they saw a dull light up ahead, like the light from a dirty bulb. It was barely enough to get them the rest of the way.

Their first steps out of the tunnel took them into a far bigger space than the glass garden. Giant rocks were scattered all around the perimeter. The growling noises were also much louder.

"Watch out!" Andrea pulled him behind one of the rocks as a group of Haggeldies approached them. "This is definitely creepy," she admitted.

"I don't think we're supposed to be here."

"We better keep our eyes open."

After eight different packs of Haggeldies had walked past them, Jacob whispered, "This must be where the Haggeldies live."

"All we've seen since we got here is Haggeldies and rocks."

"I don't get it. How can all these ugly things live so close to that beautiful garden?"

"Maybe the garden acts like camouflage—you know?" Andrea supposed. "Its beauty covers up their ugliness?"

"Speaking of ugly. . ." He poked her arm and pointed at another group headed their way. "The one in front is Aldjor. Not much to look at, is he?"

"Makes you want to throw up."

They chuckled at her comment. But when Aldjor stopped to look their way, they realized laughter stood out in a place like this. They couldn't afford to be discovered when they were so outnumbered.

Jacob crouched down and motioned for Andrea to get low as well. Staying close to the ground, they crept over to the rock immediately in front of them. Once there, they looked around for any Haggeldies who might be coming.

Andrea noticed that every Haggeldie was moving in the same direction. "We should follow them," she mouthed and pointed. When there was an opening, they did, crawling to the next rock, and then the next.

They stayed hidden and made good progress until Jacob's foot slipped on some gravel. He scurried to get behind the closest rock and pushed his back up against it as tightly as he could, but it was too late. One of the Haggeldies heard the noise and walked over to investigate.

Andrea also ducked down. Then she covered

her head with her arms to make herself as small as possible. Both of them took shallow breaths, and very few of those. They could hear the Haggeldie on the opposite side of the rock sniffing around. Every time it inhaled, Andrea's body shook, while Jacob pushed down the urge to make a run for it.

Just as the Haggeldie was about to come around to their side...

"Hey! What are you doin'?" A second Haggeldie called out.

"I thought I heard somethin' over here, maybe an outsider."

"Can't be. Nobody could get this far. Besides, we don't have time for search and destroy. We need to get to the gathering."

The first Haggeldie took one more monstrous sniff, and then stepped away. "I could swear something's not right."

As soon as the Haggeldies were out of sight, Jacob and Andrea took several enormous breaths. Then they started to move again. They made their way past a few more rocks, when Jacob pointed to his ears.

"Do you hear that?" he whispered.

"It's like a ton of animals growling."

"It's coming from over there," he pointed up ahead.

Getting as close to the uproar as they thought they should, Andrea held out her hands and boosted Jacob up on a rock. Once he was high enough to peer over the top, he almost fell back onto her because of what he saw. For less than ten feet away, standing shoulder to shoulder, were hundreds of Haggeldies.

A large, gray-haired one stepped to the center. He wore a black robe which fit strangely over the bristly lumps on his body while a stone crown sat awkwardly on his head. The rest of the repulsive creatures grunted when the elder one appeared.

"As your Supreme Leader, I demand a clear focus on our mission. Some have lost touch with the deep loathing needed to do what is necessary. It is not enough to bring trouble to our enemies. We must ruin them! We must dominate and destroy them, body, mind and spirit, till they've lost all hope and given themselves over to us completely! Then we can teach them to tap into the awesome power of hatred and bitterness. As always, our greatest enemy, The Man in the Middle—"

At the mention of his name, the Haggeldies howled. The Supreme Leader waved his arms to encourage them. Satisfied with their fervor, he calmed them down enough to be heard over the dull roar.

"Our greatest enemy teaches the Tellurians to hope in what is good. There is nothing good. He encourages them to see the best in others. But evil dwells in everyone. He tells them to set aside their anger. Yet, our anger gives us an advantage!

"We cannot allow such vile teaching to be

spread. So, I declare to you a new plan for victory. We will capture one Tellurian at a time, bring them to our lair and overwhelm them with the collective power of our hatred till they give in to the pain and, in the end, to us. After our prisoner has embraced their anger, they will help us trap other Tellurians until we rule them all. This will lead to the total defeat of the Man in the Middle!"

The Haggeldies snarled with enthusiasm over this new strategy. Jacob, on the other hand, had heard enough. If the Haggeldies were going to capture one enemy at a time, it would not be him or Andrea. He slid off the rock and motioned for her to follow him back to the glass garden where it was safe to tell her what he'd heard. Her only response was, "We need to get out of here now!"

They ran for all they were worth and didn't stop till they stood in the field with their swords in their hands.

Chapter Eighteen – A Battle Lost

Another Saturday gave Jacob another chance to hang out with his friends. But when he got to Del's house, he found Tommy alone in the front yard.

"Where's Del?"

"I don't know."

They knocked on the door and Mrs. Seliger answered. Jacob had grown to like her in spite of her quirks. She always greeted them with a smile and found something for them to eat. Today, her skin was pale, her eyes were swollen and her smile was missing.

"Are you okay, Mrs. Seliger?"

She looked beyond them and avoided the question. "Del won't be able to spend time with you today. He's not feeling well."

"Can we see him. . .to say hi?" Tommy asked.

"Only for a minute."

She led them to Del's room where he lay with the covers tucked under his chin. His skin was a light blue and his mouth hung open.

"He looks awful," Tommy whispered.

Some of Mrs. Seliger's treasures had been moved aside to make room for two chairs next to Del's bed. In one sat his father. In the other was his doctor, John L. Malson.

After an awkward silence, Jacob cleared his throat and asked, "How is he?"

"He's extremely sick, I'm afraid," Dr. Malson

replied.

"Can you give him something to make him feel better?"

"At this point, the best we can do is keep him comfortable."

Silence took over as the words sunk in. For the next several minutes, Jacob and Tommy went from staring at the floor, to looking at Del's hollow eyes, to scanning all the stuff in his room, to looking at each other and then back to staring at the floor.

Whenever Del became restless, Dr. Malson leaned forward to look him over more closely, his dad stroked his forehead, and his mom kissed his hand. No one could say if he even knew who was in the room with him until he spoke in the softest of voices. "Jacob," was all he got out.

This one word encouraged Mrs. Seliger. "Come here, Jacob. I think he wants to tell you something,"

He squeezed past her and leaned over the bed. Del's eyes opened long enough for him to whisper what only Jacob could hear.

"What did he say, son?" Del's father asked.

"'Don't give up, no matter what.'"

No one knew if Del was talking about himself or encouraging those in the room with him. As Dr. Malson wiped a tear from his cheek, Mrs. Seliger laid her face next to Del's while Mr. Seliger began to weep. Jacob shuffled back to the end of the bed.

"We need to get out of here, man," Tommy whispered. Jacob agreed. They said their good byes and Mrs. Seliger walked them to the door. "Thank you for stopping. I'm sure he appreciated it. We all did."

They nodded and hopped on their bikes. Jacob pedaled hard, the wind on his face blowing the tears off his cheeks. Once he got home, he grabbed one of his mom's gooey rolls and slumped into a chair at the kitchen table.

"You're back early." his mother noticed.

He could barely get the words out. "Del's skin was a weird color, and he just laid there in bed."

His mom put her arm around his shoulder. "It couldn't have been easy to see him that way."

"Is he ever going to get better?" He hoped she had a different answer than Dr. Malson.

"He's been sick a long time, honey. I'm not sure he'll get past this."

"It's not fair! Del never hurt anybody, not even the people who picked on him."

"You're right. It's not fair. And there's no good way to explain it. All we can do is help each other get through the bad times the best we can."

Jacob threw the roll back on the table untouched and went off for a long bike ride. When he got home, his mom said Mrs. Seliger had called. Del had passed away. Jacob wanted to bang his fists against the walls or race to Del's house to see if it was true. Instead, he just stood there, numb and helpless.

His mom wrapped her arms around him. As she stroked his head, he leaned into her, sobbing and breathing in the familiar smell of her hair.

Three days later, the whole Tannin family went to the funeral. Jacob had only been at one funeral before, for a distant relative who lived to be ninety-nine. The church was mostly empty, and everyone agreed she'd lived a good, long life. Today, hundreds of people lined up outside the church, and every one of them was certain Del's passing was senseless.

Jacob's dad gathered with other men around Del's father. They spoke in low voices and stared at the carpet. His mom joined a group of women who stood near the casket, surrounding Del's mother. They greeted each other with hugs as they cried and talked and cried some more.

Jacob found Tommy and the two of them stationed themselves near one of the stained-glass windows where they hoped to pretend this wasn't happening. He was surprised when Olivia leaned up against the wall next to them rather than standing outside on the gravel parking lot with her friends.

"I'm so sorry for your loss."

"He was always such a nice boy."

"I can't imagine how much you'll miss him."

"He was so polite."

"If there's anything I can do, don't hesitate to call."

The three of them heard all the comments

made by people going through the line along with Del's parents thanking each one for their kindness.

"What is he doing here?" Tommy pointed at Willard and his mom who were next in line.

Jacob glared at Willard, hoping to make him feel guilty.

Olivia took hold of Jacob's arm. "Let it go," she advised.

Tommy added, "There's nothing we can do."

Still, Jacob gave Willard every angry look he could generate.

During the service, songs were sung, prayers were prayed and the Pastor preached. "As people of faith, we are not immune to bad things. We live in the world like everyone else. We experience loss like everyone else. And yet, we have hope when the worst things happen because we believe there is life beyond this one, life in another world."

Jacob heard him but didn't really hear him. He was more concerned with not crying, so he counted and recounted the number of gray hairs on the head of the man in front of him till the service was over.

On the car ride home everyone was quiet. Usually, his parents would get so carried away singing along with the radio it was embarrassing. Today, Jacob wanted to hear their voices. But no one sang a single note or spoke a single word.

Once he got home, Jacob went straight to his room. He was mad about Del getting sick, mad at

Willard for being at the funeral, mad at himself for thinking Del was weird and mad about all the times he'd let Del get picked on. He laid on his bed and cried himself to sleep.

In a short time, he found himself curled up in a ball near the rock in the fence line. He climbed it to search for the Man in the Middle. He wanted answers. He would demand answers! He checked the edge of the woods and looked inside the cave. Finally, he dropped to the ground, pulled his knees to his chest and stared out at the field.

"Pretty rough, huh?" It was the Great Pine.

"Yeah."

"I wish I had magic words to take away the pain, but when things like this happen, it just hurts, that's all."

He shot an angry look at the Pine.

"Hey, I'm not trying to be cruel. If it didn't hurt, it would mean Del wasn't that important to you."

"But he was!"

"Of course, he was. So, you feel it. It's part of having a friendship worth having."

For a long time, Jacob sat there picking blades of grass, rolling them into balls and flicking them into the air while the Great Pine stood by his side. Eventually the Pine spoke.

"You're pretty good at that."

"Says the tree that doesn't have any hands." They both chuckled. "I practice with boogers." Jacob added, though he didn't know why he said such a stupid thing. Yet, it did make them laugh.

For the longest time, neither of them said anything until Jacob confessed, "I wish I'd sat by him earlier."

"At least you found out he was more than Smelly Delly."

"I was wrong to call him that."

"You did become his friend, though. And you're still his friend."

"Is it ever going to stop hurting?"

"After a while, it won't be quite as bad. Give your courage a chance to carry you through."

Jacob hugged his knees tighter as Del's last words went through his head. "Don't give up, no matter what." For the sake of his friend, he would try.

Chapter Nineteen – A Battle Won

The day after the funeral, Jacob didn't want to sit in class, listen to teachers or work on assignments. He especially didn't want to see anyone who'd called his friend "Smelly Delly."

"You don't have to go to school if you don't want to," his mom offered.

Yet, he knew he had to go back sometime. It might as well be today. Still, he wasn't prepared for how different things would be on the bus. While some of the kids goofed around like always, many were quiet. Liz didn't look up. Tommy didn't shoot spit wads. And when Willard called him short and stupid, Jacob gave him such an angry look even he backed off.

Nothing felt normal. He should have been laughing at Del's stories. Instead, he sat next to Tommy and stared out the window. That's when he heard a couple boys talking. "Hey, where's Smelly Delly?"

"Didn't you hear? He died."

"I guess he won't be stinking up our bus anymore."

That was it. He'd punch someone or yell or do something. He threw his backpack to the floor and pushed his way past Tommy. But by the time he was in the aisle, Liz had already jumped out of her seat, grabbed the ears of the guys who had mouthed off and twisted them hard.

"Don't you ever say anything like that about

Del—ever again! He was my friend. And if I hear you call him names one more time, I will take you down!"

The fear in their eyes, connected to the pain in their ears, convinced them her threat was serious. "Sorry," they spit out, hoping to save themselves. Liz gave their ears one more twist. "I mean it! Never again!" Finished with them, she turned toward everyone else, "That goes for all of you!"

The bus was quieter than ever. Even Willard kept his mouth shut. Then, Olivia started to clap. Her friends joined her, and before long, almost everyone applauded what Liz had done.

As Jacob sat down, he realized what he'd just witnessed. Haggeldies. Those guys were Haggeldies. The Man in the Middle was right. There were plenty of them in both worlds. Why hadn't he recognized all the Haggeldies who'd picked on Del every day? How come he didn't realize Liz was Del's friend? And why didn't he have the courage to say a long time ago what Liz said today?

Because the Great Pine had told him all the people in his life were more than he imagined them to be, he had gotten to know Del. Now, he looked at Liz in a new way.

In spite of the applause, Liz still sat alone. She was always by herself, same as Del had been. She didn't fit in with the other girls, who often talked about her. Her friendship with Del made sense. As the bus bumped along the uneven road, Jacob thought, "It's time to take another chance." He moved to the empty seat behind her and leaned forward. "Thanks. Those guys are creeps."

"Well, I. . .I should have done it a long time ago."

"That was pretty smart, to twist their ears. They were hurtin' for certain."

"Well," she replied in a flat tone, "The cartilage in the ear can cause great pain, especially if you have Perichondritis."

"What?"

"Oh, sorry, I forget sometimes that not everybody loves science. Perichondritis is an infection of the outer ear."

He didn't know how to respond to that, but he did learn that they thought the same way about Del. He sat back in his seat, surer than ever he needed to follow the Pine Tree's advice. It was time for Jacob the detective to work undercover once again.

Chapter Twenty – Getting to Know Her

Learning more about Liz meant sitting next to her on the ride to school, since it was the only time Jacob saw her all day. Other kids would give him grief for it, but he could minimize the damage if sitting by her looked like an accident.

He crafted the perfect plan: He'd walk down the center aisle of the bus more slowly than usual. When Liz put her legs in his way, he'd make a half-hearted attempt to push past her, pretend to trip, and then fall into the seat with her. If all went well, even she wouldn't realize he actually wanted to be there. That's how he imagined it would happen. It wasn't what happened at all.

The next day, he did move down the aisle more slowly than usual and Liz's legs did block his path. But just as he was about to "fake trip," she moved out of the way. He fell over his own feet and landed face first in her lap. Instantly, the bus broke out in laughter.

The only one without a smile was Liz, who slid out from under him while he fumbled his way to sitting up straight. And though he was tempted to tell everyone to shut up, he kept quiet. At least, he was sitting by her.

"Uh. . .sorry. I guess I'm pretty clumsy today."

"That's fine."

She looked out the window, quietly ignoring him. He had only planned how to get in the seat next to her, but he expected her to do all the talking because, in his only experience with her in the past, she had. Now he'd have to get the conversation started.

"What's going on at school today? You got any tests or projects or anything?" It sounded weird even to him.

She gave him a look like, "Who asks such a strange question?" Yet all she said was, "No, same old stuff," then went back to staring out the window.

"Umm. . .anything exciting happening at home?" This was worse than the last question!

Giving him another puzzled look, she said, "Not really."

Wow! Talking to her was nothing like he imagined. Why was she making it so difficult? Still, if he was going to learn anything about her, he'd have to try one more time.

"Are you doing anything fun this weekend?"

"No."

That was it—their whole, frustrating, dead-end conversation! How could he learn about her if she didn't talk? For the rest of the ride, he looked the other way while she stared out the window. It was time for another approach.

When Jacob got home, he dumped his backpack on the kitchen table and headed out. "I'll be back for supper!" Then he rode toward Liz's place. After he made sure the road was clear in every direction, he staked out a spot in the ditch behind a hickory nut tree, where he could spy on her without being discovered.

Liz Elliott's house was much smaller than his. There was a large clump of birch trees in the front yard and two perfectly trimmed bushes next to the house. The grass was neatly cut and freshly washed clothes hung on a line in back. Across the driveway was a weed-free garden. But no other buildings were on the property.

From where he sat, things looked perfect. Then he spotted her, standing in the garden among the sweet corn, looking in the general direction of the house.

A bald, potbellied man wearing a white t-shirt and jeans stepped onto the front porch and hollered, "Liz! Where are you?" It was her dad. "Liz! You answer me—right now!" Like another stalk of corn, she stood perfectly still. After a quick scan of the property, he went back inside, slamming the door behind him.

Within seconds, Mrs. Elliott came out. "Liz, honey, where are you?" She said in a much softer voice. "Your father and I are worried. Please come in the house."

Liz turned away, as if not looking at her mom kept her from seeing Liz.

After Mrs. Elliott went inside, Mr. Elliott started yelling. But from where Jacob stood, he couldn't make out what was being said. So he snuck up to the clump of birch trees, and from there, to the bushes next to the house. Then he crept onto the porch and crouched under the front window where he could hear every word.

"Can't you do anything right?" Mr. Elliott screamed. "My clothes were supposed to be washed, folded and put away no later than four o'clock, but no, there they are out on the line! What have you been doing all day?"

"I'm sorry. I have been trying to do what you want."

"Trying? Instead of trying, why don't you do what I say? You're useless! You don't keep up with things around here and you can't even keep track of the one child we have. If we had other kids would you lose them, too?"

Haggeldie. Liz's dad was a Haggeldie who found fault with everything.

For what seemed like forever, her dad criticized her mom. First, he grumbled about the things she failed to get done. Next, he brought up how everything she did do wasn't up to his standards. Peeking through the window, Jacob saw Liz's mom on the sofa with her hands folded in her lap and her head down. Every so often, she tucked her short, brown hair behind her ears or wiped her eyes with a handkerchief. Mr. Elliott paced the floor in front of her, stopping only to put his fist in her face.

"Look at me! Maybe if you listened to me, you wouldn't be such a lousy wife. And maybe you could do something about this homely daughter of yours. She gets average grades. She has no talent. There's nothing special about her. At least if she were pretty, I could be proud of that. Between the two of you, I can't decide which is worse. How did I end up with such a crappy family?"

The only break in the yelling was when her mom apologized or her dad stepped outside to call for her. "Liz Elliott, you get in here this instant! I will not tolerate such behavior!"

Jacob couldn't understand how married people could treat each other so badly or how a parent could run down their child the way Mr. Elliott did. He was always friendly when Jacob saw him at church. Obviously, there was more to him than he realized—and it was not good. No wonder Liz hid in the sweet corn.

"He says this kind of stuff to her all the time."

Jacob jerked his head to the right. Liz was standing at the corner of the house. He'd been caught listening in on a family secret. But before he could make an excuse for being there, she spoke.

"I need to get out of here. Want to go for a walk?"

"Sure."

They snuck across the yard, through the ditch and onto the road, away from all the noise.

"Kind of weird to find me outside your front window, huh?"

"Actually, I'm kinda glad someone else gets to see what he's like."

"What's he so mad about?"

"How would I know?" She shrugged. "His shirts weren't hung up the right way or she wasn't making what he wanted for supper. He's always angry about something."

"So he hollers at your mom other times?"

"Are you kidding? He's like this every day."

"But he seems like such a nice guy. He always smiles at me and says 'hello.'"

"Well, when other people aren't around, he's not such a nice guy."

"Sorry," He felt like someone should say it.

"It's not your fault."

"I'm just saying, I wouldn't like it if my dad was angry all the time. It would make me nervous. I'd wonder what he was going to be mad about next. But with you, it's like nothing ever gets to you."

"I'm used to hiding it."

"Does he yell at you a lot, too?"

"What do you call a lot?"

"Well, is it worse if he has a bad day? I mean, what does he say to you?" He wanted to find out if she knew how disappointed her dad was with her.

"He complains about everything. When I joined the science club, he said it was a waste of time. When I got a *B* in math, he called me stupid. He gets angry over the smallest things, like one time when the shoes in my closet weren't in a straight line. Mostly, he says I should be more like other girls, more girlie. I don't always feel like the kind of girl my dad wants me to be. And I can't talk to my mom about it. I don't want her to feel worse than she already does. I mean, he puts her down as much as he does me, and she can't stop him. What am I supposed to do?"

Her answer put an end to his questions. After all, he wasn't about to ask what it's like to have a father who isn't proud of you.

They walked in silence, taking turns kicking a small stone down the road. After they turned around at the corner, Jacob asked one more question. "Do you ever talk back to him?"

"Yeah, like that would help."

She took a deep breath. "Sometimes I do, just to hear my own voice. But it only makes him angrier and the whole thing goes on longer. So I usually keep quiet."

He had to say what he was thinking about her—what he had always thought about her. "You seem like such a strong person. No one would guess all this is going on."

"I decided to try and be happy with myself, even if he isn't."

"Soooo...does the stuff other kids say about you bother you?"

"Yeah, but nothing they say could ever match what I hear from my own dad. Besides, none of them like me anyway."

"Eh, you're not so bad."

Maybe it was the dopey way he said it or the fact he poked her on the shoulder as he did. Maybe it was just a way for her to not freak out, but for some reason, she started to laugh. It was the first time he'd ever heard her laugh, and it was a gigglier, goofier laugh than he expected her to have. It was nice.

With everything he'd learned, Jacob had a new-found respect for Liz. The things she put up with made his problems seem small.

When they got back to the hickory nut tree, he grabbed his bike and took off. But they were headed in opposite directions. He to a home where the worst that would happen was his sister teasing him, though she didn't mean it. She to a house where the yelling would go on for much of the night.

Chapter Twenty-One – Dream Stealers

After seeing what Liz dealt with, Jacob was determined to fight every Haggeldie in Telluris and Chimeran. To do this, he had to get back to training. Yet the dreams that normally took him to Chimeran weren't working. It had been a good two weeks since he'd seen Andrea or Caldwell.

He tried everything that might affect his sleep: extra pillows for comfort, warm milk to get relaxed, pushups to wear himself out. And he slept hard, but his dreams didn't get him anywhere. Desperate for answers, he skipped school to visit Dr. Malson. The doctor's office took up the entire first floor of the Snell Building, the newest, shiniest building downtown. Once there, Jacob went straight to the front desk.

"I need to see Dr. Malson right away."

"Do you have an appointment?"

"Uh, no." He'd never thought about that. "But I really need to talk to him. Please?"

"Honey, all the other people here really need to talk to the doctor, too. And they have appointments. Now, the best thing for you to do is have your parents call to schedule something. We have a few openings next week. Can you tell me what this is about?"

It would sound crazy to say he had to talk to Dr. Malson because his dreams weren't taking him to a field in the world of Chimeran and he had to get to that field because his friends were counting on him to learn how to fight Haggeldies and only Dr. Malson could help because he was the Man in the Middle. Whew! He could never tell her that.

"I saw him about a sore on my chest, and he told me if it didn't go away in a couple weeks, I should come back." He added, "He told me I could stop in any time. Can you at least tell him I'm here?"

Jacob knew the receptionist didn't believe his story as soon as she rolled her eyes. Still, he hoped the distress in his voice would be enough to gain her sympathy. She tapped a stack of papers against her desk, then sighed, "I'll see what I can do. What's your name?"

"Jacob Tannin."

"Okay, honey. Take a seat. But don't get your hopes up."

He settled for the last open chair in the waiting room between a four-year-old who somehow sniffled, cried, and coughed all at the same time and an elderly gentleman who couldn't stop shaking. He squeezed his shoulders together to avoid touching either of them.

In a short while, the receptionist waved him over to the desk.

"I can't believe it. He wants me to bring you back to his office right away. Just don't take a lot of time, honey. He's a very busy man."

She led him past several exam rooms and around a corner, stopping at the first door on the left. "Here he is." Then she turned to Jacob. "Remember, make it short and sweet!"

"Jacob, I'm surprised to see you in the middle of a school day. It must be important. What's on your mind?"

"Dr. Malson, I. . .I'm worried. I haven't been able to get back to Chimeran."

"Close the door. And lock it, too. We need privacy. After all, there are Haggeldies about. Now, have you been dreaming at all?"

"Yes, but my dreams are strange."

"Tell me about them."

"I start out in a dark place and I'm trying to move forward, like toward the field, but I can't get anywhere because these long, sticky things are all over me."

"What do they feel like?"

"Wet gummy worms."

"Do they grab onto you?"

"Yeah. How did you know?"

"I just do. Tell me, what happens after these 'wet gummy worms' grab onto you?"

"I keep trying to push my way through them, but there's too many. And the more I fight, the more they're on me until I can't move at all. That's when my dream ends."

"What you're telling me is not unexpected. Because of Caldwell and Andrea, you're gaining some skills, so the Haggeldies want to keep you out of Chimeran for a while—before you become a real threat."

"Can they do that? I mean, do they have the power to keep me from dreaming?"

"They don't, but it seems they've enlisted the help of those who do."

"Who's that?"

"The Ezors."

"The whozors?"

"The Ezors. Dream stealers. They hang in the space between you and your dreams. They're forcing you to focus on them rather than where you want to go. If they keep coming after you, your pathway to Chimeran could disappear."

"So, I'll never see Andrea and Caldwell again because of Ezors?"

"If they're successful, you may not even remember Chimeran or your friends."

"That can't happen. There has to be something I can do."

"There is, but we must act quickly."

"I'll do whatever you say."

"There are two things you need to do. First, fall asleep in a new place—somewhere you've never slept before. The Ezors have already tapped into your mind to discover the places you normally fall asleep, like at home or at a friend's house...."

"Or on the bus," Jacob added.

"Or on the bus, which means they can block your way the instant you go to sleep in those places. It makes your trip to Chimeran longer and more difficult. Falling asleep somewhere new will give you a head start. Second, you have to use a different strategy when their tentacles cling to you. You can't react at all."

"But they're gross. All I want to do is get them off me."

"Understandable. Yet no matter how slimy they are or how trapped you feel, you have to resist the urge to push them away. Keep perfectly still, with your arms at your side and your hands closed in a fist. Look straight ahead and walk through them more slowly than you've ever walked before. If you fight them at all or grab at them in the slightest, they'll hold onto you more tightly than ever. You'll have to take your time and you can't move any other part of your body besides your legs—I mean, don't even turn your head or blink your eyes. If they don't tangle themselves around you as strongly, you might be able to get to the other side."

Dr. Malson led him down the hallway past two more exam rooms and took out the key to a door marked "Office."

"Weren't we just in your office?"

"This is a special place for people in unique circumstances like yours." The door opened to what looked like a small lounge. An old TV hung in the corner and a water-marked coffee table sat in front of a plush, purple sofa. Hanging from the ceiling, one light bulb worked hard to brighten the space.

"You want me to sleep here?"

"Not quite."

The doctor pulled up on the sofa's seat cushions, which opened like a door. Then he climbed into the hole and down a ladder. Before his head disappeared, he said, "Come with me."

Jacob followed the doctor into an underground chamber. With the help of a few rays of light from the room above, he could make out a small table, two chairs and a single bed.

"Welcome to my hiding place. Haggeldies and Ezors haven't discovered it yet, which makes it the perfect starting point for you."

"If I fall asleep here, I'll be free from the Ezors?"

"Only for a short while. They'll catch up to you, eventually. Hopefully you'll be deeper into your dreams and closer to Chimeran before they do. Can you do everything I've told you?"

"I have to."

He laid down as Dr. Malson climbed back up the ladder. Before swinging the sofa seat shut, the Doctor reminded him, "Remember, move slowly—and be brave."

As the cushions fell back in place, Jacob closed his eyes. Within minutes, he was dreaming. Though his dream started in the same dark place as before, there were fewer Ezors, as Dr. Malson had promised. He crept forward, following the instructions to keep every part of his body except his legs completely still. It seemed easy until more of the Ezors fastened themselves to him. Their sleazy touch made his skin wet and clammy. The only way he could keep from freaking out was to remember the goal. *Take your time. Don't grab these things, and you'll get to Chimeran.*

With every step, more Ezors clung to him. Then, without thinking, he opened his right hand. Instantly, the slimy creatures wove themselves in and out of his fingers. He wanted to toss them aside or squeeze them till they were dead. Instead, he froze in place, allowing the Ezors to drag themselves across his face and wrap themselves around his neck.

Steady. Be brave. Don't lose your cool. He stayed in one spot several minutes, barely breathing. When the writhing Ezors relaxed, he moved forward, keeping his right hand open so they wouldn't be stirred up again if he formed it back into a fist.

Step-by-step, he made his way. It took a long time to cover even a couple of yards. But after a while, fewer Ezors hung in his face. Ten yards more and he broke through the wall of Ezors. The sun shone in the field ahead of him. He was in Chimeran! Immediately, he called out for his friends. "Andrea! Caldwell! Where are you?"

In a flash, Andrea flew out of the cave. "Jacob! You're finally here. Come with me. I think Caldwell is in trouble."

Chapter Twenty-Two – True Friends

Andrea pulled him into the cave, back by the tunnels. "See? His sword is just lying on the ground. Caldwell would never leave it in the dirt. And look at the footprints. These were made by someone wearing shoes—like Caldwell. But the rest of them were made by someone who doesn't wear shoes and is not like us at all."

She didn't need to explain. They both knew Haggeldies don't wear shoes.

"It gets worse. Check out these two marks. It's like someone got dragged by their heels. They keep going till they disappear into a tunnel."

"That's the middle tunnel," Jacob noted.

"I think he fought a group of Haggeldies and they dragged him off to their lair."

They stood still as the same thought went through their heads. The Haggeldies planned to go after one person at a time. Right now, Caldwell was that person.

"We have to go get him," Jacob declared.

"What if it's a trap?"

"Doesn't matter. We still need to rescue him."

Without hesitation or a plan, they grabbed their swords and headed toward the glass garden. They quickly moved through it into the darkness of the next tunnel. Once at the Haggeldies' lair, they hid behind the first rock they could find.

"There are hundreds of Haggeldies here," Andrea whispered. "How will we ever save Caldwell?"

"Let's find him first."

Jacob's ability to hide when playing catch and chase helped them stay out of sight as they moved through the great space.

"Look!" Andrea pointed to the back of the main room where Caldwell sat, slumped over in a chair. His arms hung at his side. His chin was buried in his chest. His clothes were torn and his wrists were chained to the wall.

"They hurt him bad," Jacob said as he started toward Caldwell. Andrea grabbed his arm and held him back.

"What are you doing?"

"We need to get him out of here before it's too late."

"Not yet. We have to make sure it's safe."

So they watched for a while and saw that even though no Haggeldies stood guard, one after another did walk past him. As they did, some poked him, others teased him and still others insulted him before moving on.

"Break out of those chains, yet buddy? Just kiddin'. It's never gonna happen!"

"You're so useless; why are we even bothering with you?"

"Moron."

"Idiot."

"Loser."

"Freak."

"You're a waste of space."

Over and over they taunted him.

"Why isn't he saying anything?" Jacob wanted to know. "That isn't like him at all."

"We have to get closer," Andrea said, "and we have to get someplace where we can see the Haggeldies before they see us."

"How about that rock over there?"

They set themselves up behind the rock Jacob pointed out. And once they were sure no Haggeldies were coming, they rushed to their friend.

Andrea kneeled in front of him and looked up into his face. "Caldwell, it's us."

"What do you want?" His voice was flat.

"We came to get you," Jacob said.

"Why?"

"You're our friend and we are not going to leave you here with these Haggeldies," Andrea said. "We just have to find a way to get rid of these chains. Then we'll walk out together."

"Don't bother. It doesn't matter."

"It matters to us!" Jacob said in a voice that was a little too loud.

"Don't you get it? It's too late."

Grunts from an approaching Haggeldie sent them back to their hiding place, cutting short their argument.

"I have never seen him give up before," Andrea whispered.

"It's like he's angry at us for coming to save him."

"Like he doesn't even want to leave."

"Hey, did you see the lump under his shirt?"

"Yeah."

"I think he's turning into one of them."

"Well, he's not a Haggeldie yet." Andrea looked across at Caldwell. "What can we do to stop it?"

"There's only one thing."

"What's that?"

"Tell him the truth."

At the next opening, they hurried back to Caldwell's side. Andrea spoke first. "Listen to me. You can't believe what they're telling you. They are your enemies. They only want to hurt you."

"We know you better than they do," Jacob added. "We can tell you the truth."

"What truth?" Caldwell snapped back. "That I have no friends or that I'll never be anything more than what I am?"

"We are your friends," said Andrea. "Trust us. Those awful Haggeldies want you to feel unloved like they do. That's why they lie about who you are."

"You are not who they say you are. You said it yourself the first time I saw you. Somewhere inside you must still believe it."

A hint of recognition flashed across Caldwell's face.

"You have to keep fighting. You have to believe you are not one of them."

"I can't do it." His head hung low.

Having hung his head many times himself, Jacob knew Caldwell needed a reason to get back up after getting beat down.

"Even if you've given up on yourself, we won't give up on you because friends stand up for each other. We believe in you, and we're going to get you out of here."

"Someone's coming," Andrea warned. One more time, they ducked behind the rock.

"You realize we're going to practically have to carry him, right? He isn't strong enough to walk out on his own," Andrea said.

"Yeah, but first we have to get him out of the chains. How are we going to do that?"

"I don't have any idea."

They sat quietly as more Haggeldies showed up to slam Caldwell.

"Hey, dork face. You better get used to the way we do things 'cause this is your home from now on."

"He's a stupid looking freak, isn't he?"

At one of the Haggeldie's insults, Andrea sat up straight. "Did you see that?"

"What?"

"Did you see what happened to the chains? I noticed it before, but I wasn't sure it was real. Every time a Haggeldie insults him, the chains glow for just a second."

"I don't get it."

"The insults make the chains thicker! It's why

they keep coming over. Every time they tell him how awful he is or how bad things are for him, the chains get stronger! Making fun of him keeps him their prisoner."

The next time a Haggeldie came over to Caldwell, Andrea and Jacob focused on the chains. And sure enough, the instant a mean word was spoken the chains glowed for a second, then grew thicker.

"That's how they're doing it! They don't need to guard him. They only need to harass him. Their words trap him."

"Great! But how does that help us?" Jacob asked.

"Don't you get it? The opposite has to be true."

"Meaning what?"

"Every time we tell Caldwell good things about himself, the chains will get weaker and he will get stronger. Our words will set him free!"

At the next opening, they raced over to try to break through the lies.

"Caldwell Rones," Jacob began, "You are a great person."

"And a good friend."

"There's nothing you can't do."

"You are a warrior."

"You are not what they say you are."

With every word, the chains did become smaller. Yet they still couldn't pull them out of the wall. Then Jacob remembered what Caldwell taught him about the power of words.

"I know what to do." Getting on his knees, he lifted Caldwell's head. "You've got to help us!"

"I can't do anything."

"Yes you can. You can set yourself free from these chains."

"No I can't. Wouldn't I have already done it if I could?"

"You haven't because you've accepted what they've told you. If you don't believe me, believe what you said to me. You told me my words have power. Well, yours do, too."

Caldwell shrugged.

"You said it's up to us which words we believe. You can believe what we're telling you instead of what they say. Come on, you can do this."

They kept speaking words of encouragement while Caldwell did his best to believe what they told him. With each word, the chains glowed and became thinner. Yet they still couldn't pull them out of the wall.

The next time they hid behind the rocks, Andrea stated the obvious. "We have to do something else."

"No, we have to say something else."

When they returned to Caldwell's side, Jacob spoke. "You are perfect in every way!" Caldwell lifted his head. The words stirred something inside him.

Andrea chimed in, "Caldwell, you are perfect in every way."

"It's true," Jacob added. "You are perfect in

every way."

As they continued to speak these simple words, the chains got smaller and weaker. It was time to give it one more shot.

"On the count of three," Andrea said. They pulled so hard that when the chains came out of the wall, they both ended up on their backs. But Caldwell was free.

He was too exhausted to stand up though, so Jacob and Andrea knelt on either side of him, put his arms over their shoulders and dragged him to their hiding place. "We can't stay here and wait for some Haggeldie to come along," Andrea warned. They each took a few deep breaths and began moving from one rock to the next as quickly as they could. Finally, they entered the tunnel which would take them back toward the cave; while behind them, the Haggeldies sounded the alarm.

"The prisoner's gone! Find him. Make him pay!"

By the time they dragged Caldwell through the darkest part of the tunnel and entered the glass garden, the Haggeldies had almost caught up to them.

"We're too slow," Andrea said.

"We'll all be prisoners now," Caldwell moaned.

"I've got an idea," Jacob said.

They set Caldwell on a glass bench, then picked up figurines from everywhere in the garden. They piled them in the tunnel's opening, creating a road block of sorts.

"Won't the Haggeldies be able to just push these aside?" Andrea wondered.

"Not before it freaks em out."

And sure enough, when any of the Haggeldies got close to the figurines, they gasped, shrieked and ran the other way as their own image was reflected back on them.

"I guess we're not the only ones who think they're disgusting," Jacob chuckled.

The Haggeldies' dilemma became the three friends' opportunity to get through the next part of the tunnel. They shuffled along, supporting Caldwell every step of the way until, with their last bit of strength, they pulled him out into the woods. But by now the Haggeldies were almost on top of them and none of them had the energy for a fight.

Jacob called out, "Great Pine, we need you!"

Within seconds, the Great Pine Tree planted itself nearby.

"Haggeldies are after us! Can you fight them off?"

"I can do something better." The Great Pine lifted its branches. "Hide under here." Then it draped itself over them like a protective shield.

In a flash, dozens of angry Haggeldies rushed into the woods. When they couldn't find the three friends, they shouted their threats to the sky.

"You better watch your backs."

"We'll track you down and smash you to bits."

"You're never going to be safe." Then, they were gone.

Meanwhile, the three friends held tight to the trunk of the Great Pine.

Chapter Twenty-Three – What Really Happened

Caldwell trembled as he explained. "I was just warming up for our next practice when five Haggeldies came out of the tunnel and jumped me. I never even saw them. One of them grabbed my sword and threw it on the ground. The rest grabbed me and dragged me to their lair. I tried to fight them, but they were too strong. They grunted and gloated the whole time."

"It sounds like there was no way to stop them," Andrea said.

"When we got there, hundreds of them pushed up against me. They stunk so bad I thought I'd puke! Then a fat, old Haggeldie in a black robe stood over me. When he raised his hands and started to talk, it got real quiet."

"What did he say," Jacob asked.

"Something like, 'Our plan for victory begins with this one worthless Tellurian! Today, we break his will and turn him into one of us. He imagines he's powerful. Even now, he looks for a way to escape. Yet he's already lost.'

"Then he twisted my head and forced me to look at the ceiling. He told me there was a power above me I couldn't overcome, a power that draws all Haggeldies together."

"What was it?" Jacob asked.

"This huge rock. It was right on top of me. He

asked if I could feel the power of 'the Rock of Oppression.' He said it made their hatred stronger. I can't explain it, but it felt like my chest was being crushed.

"Then he said nothing would ever get better for me, so I might as well get it over with and become one of them. He said, 'Call on the Rock of Oppression to fill you with rage. Embrace your anger. Learn how to hate.'

"The rest of them went crazy—jumping around, screaming and howling while the one in the black robe laughed. Then he told them to shut up so he could pray to the rock."

"What kind of prayer would a Haggeldie say?" Jacob asked.

"It was like. . .'O great Rock of Oppression, accept our offering. Give us strength to crush our enemies and fill us with the hatred that overcomes good.'"

"Wow, that's weird and creepy," Andrea said.

"After that, they chained me to the chair where you found me. Even there I could feel the weight of that stupid rock." His eyes watered.

"It wasn't your fault," Andrea told him. "There were too many of them."

"You did your best," Jacob added. "Besides, the Man in the Middle says no one wins all their battles. At least now it's over."

"But it's not over. I was lucky. You came to save me. But when someone else is taken, who will rescue them?"

"We need to stop the Haggeldies before they capture anyone else," Andrea declared.

"We can't do that. There's only three of us."

"Not true," said the Great Pine. "There are many more who struggle with Haggeldies every day. Any of them would be glad to join you. And don't forget me and my friends. We're on your side."

Liz and Tommy immediately came to Jacob's mind. "The Great Pine's right. There are others like us."

"If we can get them to Chimeran, we can train them to be warriors," Andrea resolved.

"Then," Caldwell added, "we can attack the Haggeldies before they come after us."

With a plan in place, they went off on a new mission to find all the warriors they could.

Chapter Twenty-Four – The Truth about Dreams

Liz and Tommy were perfect recruits for the army of warriors, yet there was so much Jacob needed to tell them before he could ask them to join the fight. And none of it would be easy.

Of course, he'd recount the adventures he'd had and the new friends he'd made. He'd describe what Haggeldies looked like, how they acted, and how dangerous they were. But he'd also have to find a way to explain how his dreams took him to another world. All this would already make him sound crazy before he even had a chance to convince them a war was coming.

On top of everything else, he'd have to get them to accept that his experiences in Chimeran had started him on the path to becoming a courageous warrior. How could they believe he was brave enough to fight in an epic battle against enemies they'd never seen in a world they'd never been to when day after day they watched him back down from Willard? For their sake, for Chimeran and for himself this needed to change.

That afternoon, as he got on the bus, Jacob didn't stare at the floor or rush to his seat. Instead, he kept his head up and took firm, even steps down the aisle till he stood in front of Willard.

With an expression that was more sneer than smile, Willard gave a loud laugh. "Hey, short and stupid is here. Did somebody leave your cage open or are ya just makin' it easy for me to hit ya? Well—say somethin'! Otherwise, get outta my face, dipwad."

Jacob gripped and released the straps on his backpack as he stared at Willard's fat cheeks. Part of him wanted to race to his seat and forget about standing up to him—yet, another part of him had had enough of being pushed around. With one long breath, he forced the words out. "I want you to quit calling me names. I am not short and I am not stupid."

"No, you're stupider than I thought." Willard roared as he got up. "Only a dummy would try to tell me what to do. You'll be shorter, too, once I pound you into the ground."

Could everyone hear his heart bang against his rib cage? He took another deep breath and reminded himself, *He's just like any other Haggeldie. Don't listen to what he says. Believe in yourself. Your words have power.*

"I want you to stop hitting me, too—and bending my fingers back and picking on me." He told himself to breathe as he kept his eyes on Willard.

Red faced, Willard didn't make a move. Instead, he stared over Jacob's shoulder. *What is he looking at?* Jacob turned to see the other kids stand up, one by one. Together, they glared at

Willard. *So this is what an army of warriors looks like.*

Finally, Willard announced, "I got better things to do than bother with this loser. You're not worth my time." Then he sat down.

In that moment, Jacob realized Willard was afraid of the world around him like every Haggeldie is. He nodded at Willard to cement their new understanding. When he turned to walk back to his seat, he saw the others still on their feet and smiled.

"That was awesome, man." Tommy said. "Though I was pretty sure he was going to pound you. He could have, too. . .whenever he wanted. You know that, right?"

"Yeah."

"So why'd you do it?"

"I'm tired of all the stuff he pulls."

Tommy shook his head in amazement while Liz gave him a thumbs up.

"Hey, guys, I need to tell you something really important. But we can't talk here. Meet me in the woods behind Tommy's house later."

"What's the big secret?" Tommy asked.

"I can't say till we're alone. The wrong people might hear us."

"I love secrets," Liz said. "I'll be there."

"I got nothin' else to do," Tommy added.

Around four o'clock, they gathered in the woods. Liz and Tommy sat on a fallen tree while he paced back and forth in front of them.

"Okay, here goes. Do you guys have dreams?"

"Seriously?" Tommy said. "You couldn't ask this on the bus?"

"Okay. . ." He paused before trying again. "What I mean is do your dreams ever feel like they're real? Like what's happening in them is as real as us being here in this woods? 'Cause mine do."

"Didn't you tell me this same thing like a long time ago? I thought that was weird, but making us come all the way out here to say it is even weirder."

"My dreams feel that way sometimes," Liz interrupted.

"Good, 'cause the last few months, I've learned something about my dreams. It'll sound crazy, but don't say anything till I'm done, okay?"

They listened as he told them about his first sword fight with Andrea and watching Caldwell defeat five Haggeldies at one time. He described what Haggeldies look like, as well as The Man in the Middle, the Great Pine Tree, the Little People, the glass garden—even the dog on the farm. He also told them about the mirrors rising out of the ground, the Pine Tree comforting him after Del's death, he and Andrea rescuing Caldwell from the Haggeldies' lair and seeing his Great-aunt Polly.

"Are you done yet?" Tommy asked.

"Not quite. What I'm about to tell you is going to be the hardest part for you to believe. I met these people and had these experiences in a place called Chimeran. Our dreams take us there. It's a real world where we live another part of our life."

He'd done it. And it had gone pretty well except for Liz's eye roll near the end. "What do you think?"

Tommy didn't hesitate. "You're mental. You want us to believe we live part of our lives here on earth and another part in a place called Chimeran?"

"Yeah. Except in Chimeran they don't call this earth, they call it Telluris."

"Whatever. It doesn't sound right to me. Maybe you're dreaming now?"

Liz tried harder to be kind. "I want to believe what you're telling us. I do. Some of my dreams feel like they actually happened. But another world and all these people and Haggeldies? There's no scientific evidence for anything you're telling us. Maybe you just have a better imagination than we do."

"It's not my imagination, Liz. Chimeran is real! You have to trust me. There's a lot at stake. Otherwise I wouldn't have told you anything about it. I need your help."

To make his case, Jacob shared how he found a scab on his arm the morning after he'd been cut by Andrea and how he was tired the morning after the Great Pine chased him around the house.

"Dude, you scratched yourself 'cause you were having a wild dream," Tommy explained. "Big deal. And haven't you seen dogs move their legs in their sleep, like they're running? But they don't go anywhere. You can see them right there, on the floor, dreaming. That's what you were doing, dreaming. You didn't go to another world. You never even left your bed."

"Don't you remember how I complained about having sore arms? They hurt because I'd been swinging a heavy sword while I was training for combat."

Then, he made his final pitch. "I'm only telling you because a battle is about to take place and we can't win it without you."

After he laid out the Haggeldies' plan, he begged them, "I need you, all my friends in Chimeran need you. If you don't join the fight, bad things will happen for everybody."

"I don't know," Liz said.

"I'm telling you, it's all true, including the Haggeldies! You've seen them yourself."

"I've never seen a Haggeldie." Tommy said.

"You've seen them every day—in class, on the bus, in your own home. You've even done battle with them."

They looked at each other and shrugged their shoulders.

"Okay, Liz, what about the two guys on the bus who shot off their mouths about Del? You grabbed 'em by the ears to shut them up. Those were Haggeldies. And Tommy, remember the guy in the cafeteria who knocked the tray out of your hands? When you went to pick it up, he pushed you to the ground. He was a Haggeldie. Or how about the people who always complain about you or put you down? Are you going to tell me those people aren't in your life? Those are Haggeldies, real-life Haggeldies we face every day!"

"You've lost it, man," Tommy said.

Liz also struggled to make sense of it. "I get it. There are bad people who hurt others, but calling them Haggeldies and saying they exist in another world where a huge war is about to happen? Sounds like you're not dealing with reality. Maybe you should see a psychologist or a doctor or someone."

His face lit up. "That's it!"

"What's it?"

"We should go see a doctor."

"Dude, she meant you, alone, therapy, hopefully some good drugs."

"No, no. It'll help. We'll go to Dr. Malson's office. He'll explain everything!"

"What would Dr. Malson know about this?" Liz asked.

"More than anybody. He's the Man in the Middle."

With that news, they almost fell off the tree.

The next afternoon, the three of them ditched school and headed to the doctor's office. As soon as the receptionist saw him, she threw her hands in the air. "I know, honey. You don't have an appointment, but Dr. Malson will want to see you anyway. Have a seat. I'll tell him you're here. I assume he's going to want to see your two little friends as well?"

"Yes, please, ma'am."

In a matter of minutes, she led them to the doctor's office. "Liz. Tommy, come in. It's good to see you. I was hoping you'd get here eventually."

"How do you know my name?" Liz asked.

"You'd be surprised how much I know about each of you. That's not why you're here though, is it? Jacob, you better close the door again."

Once he sat down, Jacob explained. "I told them about my dreams, about everything so I could recruit them for the war against the Haggeldies. They think I'm making it up."

"Well, well. . .you've brought me quite a challenge. Think back, Jacob. How much did you have to go through and how many people had to explain things to you before you believed Chimeran or Haggeldies or anything else was real? You had your doubts, didn't you? In fact, you were pretty stubborn about it."

"Yeah."

"So, give them a chance. You can't expect them to accept it just because you say it. They have to experience it."

"You mean he's telling the truth?" Liz asked.

"He's not really good at lying, is he?"

"No," she replied with a smile.

"Think of it this way. We all have dreams, good ones, bad ones, dreams we remember, dreams we don't. Imagine the world you could create if you mixed together all the dreams every person has!"

"I can fly in some of mine," Tommy offered. "Then, sometimes when I'm trying to get away from a monster, it feels like my feet are stuck in mud."

"We all have those dreams. We also have other ones which belong only to us. Don't you dream about what your life will be in the future? Don't you dream about every awful thing in your life going away?"

With each question, they nodded their heads.

"Sometimes our dreams frighten us, other times they give us hope. Jacob is telling you our dreams all happen in another world and our dreams take us to that world."

In a soft tone that was out of character, Liz spoke. "Sometimes, when I first fall asleep, a voice whispers, 'Your life isn't what you want it to be, but I won't let you get lost.' It's almost like a dream, and it helps me feel better."

"You left out the other thing the voice whispers," the doctor said. "'I'll always be with you.'"

"How did you know that? I never told anybody."

"Because the dream world Jacob's talking about is real. Just think. If the hopes and dreams you carry inside you every day are real, why can't a dream world be real as well? He's not lying.

Chimeran exists. He's also not lying about Haggeldies. They are your enemies—both here and there."

"So are you the Man in the Middle Jacob's been talking about?" Tommy asked.

"In Chimeran I am. . .let's just say I'm more than you see here today, like you're more than what other people see. The world of Chimeran helps us discover who we truly are."

Dr. Malson leaned forward on his desk. "Jacob, they need to see it in order to understand. Why don't you meet them there tonight? Let them explore the place."

"How can they get to a place they've never been before? A place they don't even believe exists?"

"Who says they haven't been to Chimeran?"

"We have?" Liz and Tommy exclaimed.

"You may not remember it, but yes, you have. As far as the three of you meeting there, it's going to take teamwork."

"But there is a way, right? I mean, you wouldn't suggest it if you didn't already have a plan, would you?"

"You're getting to know me."

Liz was on the edge of her seat. "Please, tell us. What can we do?"

"Tonight, all three of you must go to bed at precisely ten o'clock. While lying there, you need to think about each other and where you want to be as you repeat these words: 'I'm going to meet my friends in Chimeran. . .I'm going to meet my friends in Chimeran.' This is important. You must keep saying these words until you fall asleep. If you stop, even for a second, the enchantment won't be as effective. Jacob, you'll need to give them an exact description of the place. They have to be able to imagine it in detail while they say the words."

"And this will work?"

"I'm not promising anything, but if you don't try, they'll never believe what you're telling them."

The doctor was right. So Jacob described the field, the woods and the entrance to the cave. "We'll meet by the rock in the fence line tonight."

Chapter Twenty-Five – Chimeran

"Jacob! I'm by the rock. Jacob! Where are you?" Liz called out. "Jacob!"

"I'm over here!"

Her eyes got big as he ran toward her from the road. "This field, that rock, the woods—everything is just the way you described it."

He could only grin.

"Did you see Tommy yet?" she asked.

"No, but he's got to be here somewhere."

They ran toward the woods, calling his name as they went. "Tommy! Tommy Leaver! Come on. Show your face." Before long, he poked his head out from the cave's entrance.

"Wow! It's cool down there."

"See? I was telling the truth."

Liz pinched her arm, stomped her feet on the ground and rubbed her hand against the bark of a tree. "It feels pretty real."

Jacob stretched out his arms, "Friends, welcome to Chimeran! Let me show you around." He pointed out the neighbor's farm and the dog he'd named Red. He took them to the tunnels at the back of the cave, warning them not to enter any on their own. And from there, he led them into the woods to introduce them to the Great Pine. They agreed it looked exactly like the tree near his house, except this one spoke.

"Tommy, Liz, good to see you."

"How are you doing, uh, Piney? Can I call you

Piney?" asked Liz.

Jacob let out a laugh. "Are you scared to talk to a tree?"

"It's my first time, give me a break."

"Ignore him, Liz. He's forgetting how afraid he used to be around me. But you don't have to worry. I'd never hurt you. And you can call me Piney any time you want—but only you."

"Can all the other trees talk?" Tommy asked.

"Of course. Come on, I'll introduce you."

"Sorry, no time." Jacob pulled them away and continued the tour. It ended with the three of them standing on top of the rock.

"It's so peaceful here," Liz said. She'd barely gotten the words out when the sky rumbled. It sounded like thunder, but not quite thunder, for mixed in with the rumbling was a gravelly voice.

"Horse-face Liz. I see why your dad is disappointed in you. You're more than plain. You're plain nasty. Do you practice being ugly? Too bad cause girls who look like you don't matter as much as the pretty ones. You're not too bright, either, are you? At least if you were smart, that would be something. You really let him down."

She wiped the tears off her face with her sleeve. "Why is he saying those things?"

"It's a Haggeldie. It's what they do. Don't listen to it or to any other Haggeldie," Jacob explained. "They're all liars. He just wants to make you feel bad. But you can choose what you think about yourself."

A second voice spoke through the thunder. "And Tommy, what a sorry little person you are. You think your wisecracks are funny? People only laugh because you sound like a jerk. They're laughing at you. And everybody knows you make those stupid comments to cover up how sad you are. It's not working. Otherwise you'd have better friends than these two—the loser and the homely one. There was Smelly Delly, but he's dead, so he doesn't count anymore."

Tommy stared straight ahead, pretending the words didn't bother him. Again, Jacob spoke up. "Don't let it get to you. Haggeldies make things up all the time. Just because they say it doesn't make it true."

"Really Jacob?" The rumbling went on, only this time the voice was Aldjor's. "These two are your best hope? Ha, ha, ha, ha. This shows how desperate you are. But they won't be any help. We've defeated them before—many times. When will you realize what a loser you are, what a loser you'll always be and what loser friends you have?"

Jacob didn't hesitate to fight back with his own words. "Everything you said is a lie! My friends are strong and smart and they never give up. And. . .and. . .you have no power over us!"

Jacob's rant quieted the sky and drove the Haggeldies away. "Guys, forget what those things said. They're just messing with you. You're not like that. There are all sorts of good things about you."

Tommy and Liz were still rattled, but at least they understood what made this enemy dangerous and the upcoming battle necessary.

"They are awful, horrible creatures," Liz said. "I'll be glad to fight them."

Tommy agreed. "Me too."

"Then come with me cause you need to start your training right away."

Chapter Twenty-Six – The Gathering of Friends

The rest of their time in Chimeran was spent with a sword in their hands. And for the next several weeks, the three of them went there regularly to train with Andrea and Caldwell. Liz was a natural. Tommy, on the other hand, was clumsy. If the sword didn't get knocked out of his hands, he dropped it on his own or tripped over it.

"Come with me, Liz," Andrea said. "We need to get away from these guys and do some real sword work."

"What does that mean?" Tommy asked.

"Eh, she thinks girls are better swordfighters than guys," said Caldwell. "WHICH THEY'RE NOT!" The girls were long gone by the time he'd shouted it.

"I need to check something out," Jacob said. "You guys stay here and practice." By the time he'd returned, Andrea and Liz had come back as well.

"Where did you go?" Tommy asked.

"To the farm. The one you can see from the top of the rock."

"You know, we don't have time for field trips," Andrea added. "We're supposed to plan for a battle...and practice for it."

"I just wanted to ask about the rock."

"What did the farmer say?" Caldwell asked.

"It's been there as long as he can remember. He tried to dig it out once, but gave up 'cause it was too big."

"What does that have to do with anything?" Andrea was annoyed.

"Don't you get it?"

All four friends shook their heads "No."

"The rock in the fence line has to be the Rock of Oppression."

"Even if you're right, it doesn't help us," Caldwell said. "The Haggeldies get power from the rock. We get nothing."

"What if there's a way we can use it to our advantage? We need to talk to the Great Pine."

"Oh, Piney," Liz called out.

Huddled under the Great Pine's branches, Jacob explained what he had in mind. They all agreed it was worth a shot, and the Great Pine vowed the trees would do their part.

After three more weeks of training, everything was in place for an attack on the Haggeldies' lair. On the day of the battle, Jacob, Liz and Tommy waited outside the cave—eager to see how many other recruits Andrea and Caldwell had found. In a matter of minutes, hundreds came out of the woods to join them in the field.

"How did you get all these guys to show up?" Jacob asked.

"We told people who told other people," Andrea explained.

Jacob called them together. "Hey, everybody. I'm Jacob and I'm here to fight back against the Haggeldies because I'm tired of being told I can't do anything right, and I'm sick of being pushed around. How about the rest of you?"

They all shouted and cheered and nodded their heads in agreement. Then Andrea prepared them for what they would face.

"Be ready for the very worst because Haggeldies will say or do anything to hurt you. Do not listen to them, no matter what. And always keep track of those who are around you. If someone goes down, help them get back up. Count on each other. Your strength and courage, added to theirs, will give us the victory!"

She lifted her sword high in the air and let loose with her signature cry, "Aieee! Aieee!" Soon, all the warrior friends joined her. "Aieee! Aieee! Aieee!"

Jacob could see the determination on each face. Every warrior was ready for battle, even the girl who stepped out from the back of the crowd to say in her familiar voice, "Hi, bro."

"Olivia? Wha. . .what are you doing here?"

"Did you think you were the only dreamer in the family?"

"You didn't tell me you knew about Chimeran."

"The Man in the Middle said you needed to learn on your own. If you knew I was here, you might have stopped coming to the field and you'd never be strong enough to fight Haggeldies."

"I don't get it. You're popular. Nothing bad ever happens to you."

Olivia laughed. "Are you kidding? I get put down all the time. You just never noticed."

Even she's more than I thought she was, he realized.

Caldwell interrupted. "Everybody's ready. We need to go."

Jacob gave the orders. "Trees to the fence line. Warriors, follow me."

Weapons in hand, they headed toward the cave. But before they could get to the entrance, a tremendous rush of wind pushed them backwards. This wind was created by hundreds of Little People who flew out of the woods and either landed on the warrior friends or settled into one of the trees. And the flood of Little People was followed by Great-aunt Polly.

"I hear you're taking on the Haggeldies."

Lying on the ground, with several Little People on top of him, Jacob responded, "That's the plan."

"Not without us!"

"Uh. . .no offense, Aunt Polly, but these guys are tiny! How can they make a difference in a battle with big, ugly Haggeldies? They'll get squashed!"

She laughed. "They knocked you down, didn't they? Besides, haven't you learned not to judge others by what you see on the outside? You can't measure the size of their hearts by looking at the size of their bodies! Trust me. These Little People can do more than you imagine. You need them."

"I'm not sure I can keep them from getting hurt."

"They'll take care of themselves. Why are we even having this conversation? They're going with you, end of discussion."

He'd never won an argument with Aunt Polly before, so he quit trying to win this one. "Okay, but I still think they'll get in the way."

Aunt Polly put her finger to her lips. "Listen."

A buzzing sound filled the air. At first, Jacob thought it was the Little People flapping their wings. But they were already sitting on someone's shoulder or perched in the branch of a tree. Then he heard the words of encouragement they whispered.

"You are strong."

"You are brave."

"You're not alone."

"You can do this."

A quiet confidence came over the warrior friends as they took to heart what the Little People told them.

"See what I mean?" Aunt Polly said, "They're making a difference already."

Jacob nodded and called out once more. "Everyone to your places! Trees to the fence line. Warriors to the tunnel. Little People on board. We're off to the Haggeldies' lair!"

Chapter Twenty-Seven – A Crushing Battle

The line of warrior friends advanced through the glass garden and into the dark tunnel. Once they entered the great space the Haggeldies called home, they worked their way around the edge and hid behind the large rocks. Every warrior ended up with their back against the wall, a sword in their hands and at least one of the Little People on their shoulders. From here, they could see the person to the left and to the right of them.

Jacob raised his sword to signal the battle was about to begin. Those nearby raised theirs as well—and so on around the circle till all swords were lifted high. One of the Little People followed with a high-pitched "Whoop!" The rest joined in till the space was filled with their shouts. "Whoop Whoop! Whoop!"

The uproar did what it was meant to do as the Haggeldies rushed to the center of the room. The warrior friends then stepped out from behind the rocks to confront them. But this surprise move didn't give them the advantage they thought it would since the Haggeldies didn't back away or hesitate for even a second. Instead, they spun around in a fury, like dogs chasing their tails. To avoid getting cut by the Haggeldies' hair, the warriors were forced back toward the wall.

The Haggeldies came at them with their

swords now. They also started a war of words with the Little People:

"You're finished!"

"Don't listen to them!"

"We'll squash you and these flying bugs."

"Take the fight to them!"

"Get ready to feel some pain!"

"Don't be afraid."

Pushed into a tight space, the warriors had no room to properly swing their swords—not until Caldwell attacked the Haggeldie directly in front of him. After he broke through the line, those around him were able to gain some ground as well.

Angrier and even more aggressive, the Haggeldies pushed back in a big way. This time Andrea re-energized the Warriors with her battle cry, "Aieee! Aieee!" This put the enemy on its heels once again. And so, the conflict went back and forth between the two sides.

The first warrior to hit the ground was Tommy. As soon as he was down, one Haggeldie knocked the sword from his hand while two others stomped on him. Liz charged full speed into the first Haggeldie, who, in turn, crashed into the other two. They all landed hard, which gave Tommy time to recover his sword and return to the fight. "Thanks, man."

After what seemed like hours, the warriors made their biggest push, forcing the Haggeldies together under the Rock of Oppression. For the first time victory seemed possible. Yet the Supreme Leader took their position as a sign of hope.

"Look up, my friends, look up! We're united under our beloved Rock! Draw on its power. Fill yourself with hatred!! We cannot lose."

Equipped with a fresh supply of rage, the Haggeldies growled and yelped, then charged the warriors, who stumbled backwards. Many landed on the floor in the rush. Andrea, herself, tripped over someone who was down. Three Haggeldies were on her in an instant. Lying on her back, she swung her sword furiously in an attempt to hold them off.

At Aunt Polly's command, Little People rushed to her side. They stabbed the Haggeldies' feet and ankles with their small swords. Then they flew in the Haggeldie's faces, harassing the enemy long enough for Andrea to get back on her feet.

The warriors' lack of experience showed in this latest assault. Those who didn't get stuck against the wall got shoved to the floor. Those who hadn't lost their swords had no room to swing them.

Jacob was focused on the Haggeldie straight ahead of him when a wretched sound echoed through the lair. "Raaaggh!" "Raaaggh!" His head turned left, right, then left again as he searched for its source. Suddenly, Aldjor shoved the Haggeldie Jacob was fighting aside and declared, "This one's mine!"

Jacob had always expected to go one on one with Aldjor. But he never imagined that Aldjor would bring a new weapon to their fight. Shaped like an oar, it had a wooden handle on one end and a sharp blade attached to the other. With Aldjor's first swing of this battle-blade, Jacob's sword went flying. From then on, he could only duck and dodge to avoid being cut. As he moved side to side, he was also forced to retreat until he felt the cold rock wall against his back.

"It's time to finish you." Aldjor grunted.

Jacob was out of space and out of moves when a voice in his head whispered, *Run.* No. He'd be abandoning his friends. *Run away,* the voice insisted. No. He had to stand up to Aldjor. *Run away now!* Aldjor wound up for another blow. He'd be cut for sure.

Clang! Olivia's sword knocked the battle-blade out of Aldjor's hands. "Run!" she yelled. This time he listened.

Aldjor chased him in and out of the rocks as well as in between the warriors and the other Haggeldies. Jacob outran him more easily than he did the hornets. But when he stopped to see how far back Aldjor was, he also saw the damage Aldjor was doing. In his all-out pursuit of Jacob, he smashed into everything in his path. He sent swords flying and knocked both warriors and Haggeldies to the ground. Jacob immediately formed a new plan.

He'd stay just far enough ahead of Aldjor to

make him think he had a chance to catch up and he'd always run between a warrior and a Haggeldie.

With every pass they made around the lair, more weapons flew, more bodies fell and Aldjor grew more out of control. The destruction he caused disrupted much of the fighting.

"Whoomph!" A Haggeldie blasted Jacob from the side. His shoulders hit the rocks hard. As he struggled to get back on his feet, Aldjor dove forward to grab his ankle. "I knew I'd get you," he snarled. Jacob tried to break free by kicking with his other foot, but Aldjor's grip was too strong. He held onto Jacob with one hand and reached for a sword with the other. He was ready to strike when a new sound shook the cave from above.

Boom, boom, boom!

Instantly, Jacob called out, "Destroy the rock! Destroy the rock!" The other warriors picked up his chant, "Destroy the rock, destroy the rock!"

The Haggeldies screamed back, "You'll never destroy it!"

Aldjor stopped his attack on Jacob and joined the howling. "The Rock's power will crush you!"

Still, the pounding became stronger and louder. Its constant beat overpowered the shouts of both the Haggeldies and the warriors.

As tree roots poked through the ceiling, the Supreme Leader cried out in horror, "Haggeldies, unite! We must defend the Rock of Oppression!"

The Haggeldies ignored the warriors and

gathered directly under the rock. There, they shrieked and grunted and jumped, desperate to cut off the roots with their swords. But the squatty creatures could only get inches off the ground.

"Destroy the rock, destroy the rock," the warriors kept chanting.

"All is lost!" the Supreme Leader wailed. The rest of them also moaned in despair while clumps of dirt fell on their heads. "Nothing can save us."

Before the trees made their final push, which would cause the Rock to crash down into the Haggeldies' lair, Andrea, Jacob and Caldwell led the warriors through the tunnel and back out onto the field. Once the Rock fell, the trees pushed dirt into the hole where it had been, and the Great Pine settled into the spot.

As the Little People celebrated and the warriors slapped each other on the back, Jacob gave Tommy a high five. "Did that just happen?"

"Yeah, man!" Tommy yelled.

Liz hugged them both. "We did it."

Jacob looked up to see the Man in the Middle moving through the crowd towards him.

"Did you see it?" Jacob asked.

"I saw it all."

"Even the end, where the Haggeldies got crushed by the Rock?"

"They didn't get crushed."

"They had to. The rock came down right where they were."

"Before it hit the ground, they rushed to the edge of the lair."

"So they got away?"

"Not at all. The Rock pinned them against the wall. They're trapped by their own hatred. And they'll be stuck there a long time. It's not easy to escape feelings that strong."

"Will they come after us again?"

"If any Haggeldie does, you can handle them, right?"

Jacob nodded while the Man in the Middle moved on. Then he quietly looked at all those who had fought by his side. *Maybe I am worth something after all.*

Chapter Twenty-Eight – Something More

Little People flittered back and forth between the trees and the warriors, saying their goodbyes, while Aunt Polly pulled Jacob and Olivia aside. "I hope you'll remember how special you are to me, even when I don't remember you at the nursing home."

"Will we see you again, Aunt Polly?" Jacob asked. "I mean, in Chimeran?"

"You never know." Her eyes sparkled. "We might have more fun sometime."

She hugged them once again, and then headed into the woods. With a whoosh, the Little People followed. All the other warrior friends scattered as well, leaving only Jacob, Andrea and Caldwell standing near The Man in the Middle.

"I'm so proud of you all," he said. "You stood up for each other and you never gave up, even when things went against you. And in your own way, you showed who you are.

"Andrea, you're a natural leader. You inspire people to do their best. You are perfect in every way. Caldwell, you teach people how to stand up for themselves. After all, you understand how much determination it takes! You are perfect in every way.

"And Jacob, you've come a long way from the first time we met. Back then, you cringed at the very sight of a Haggeldie. And you couldn't use a sword to save your life! Today you showed the courage which has always been in you. You are perfect in every way."

"I'm not perfect in every way," he protested. "I get afraid. I only think about myself. I judge others without giving them a chance. And I haven't always been there for my friends."

"You still don't realize what it means when someone says this about you, do you? When I tell you that you're perfect in every way, I'm not saying you have no flaws. Everyone does. I'm saying that the people who love you see how special you are even when you don't. They see your flaws, but they look past them because they care about you."

Andrea and Caldwell put a hand on his shoulder and Jacob allowed himself the hint of a smile, though he kept his head down.

"It's a lot to take in, isn't it? But it's okay to feel good about yourself and what you've accomplished. It's okay to look down, too— because truly brave people know that being humble is not the same as being weak."

"You think I was brave?" He looked the Man in the Middle in the eyes.

"I do." He nodded. "I do."

"It was a great battle, wasn't it?" Now Jacob's smile stretched across his face.

"It was. And it showed that you're ready for something more."

"What do you mean, something more?"

"Do you remember how you lost to the Haggeldies early on, how they stomped on you and left you lying on the ground?"

"Oh yeah."

"When I showed up, what did I tell you?"

"To get up and to never give up."

"That's right. Do you also remember how you responded to my advice?"

"Kind of. . ." His face got red.

The Man in the Middle chuckled. "Your exact words were, 'You mean the only advice you have for me when I've just given up is to not give up?' A bit sarcastic, but then, sarcasm has always been part of your charm."

"If you call that charming," Andrea teased.

"Sorry. I wasn't really mad at you. I was mad at myself for letting the Haggeldies push me around."

"It's tough to figure out how to stand up for yourself. Besides, you were going through a lot. I'm only bringing it up because you also said, 'There has to be something more than this!' And what did I tell you?"

"You said there was, but I wasn't ready for it yet."

"You weren't. You were angry and frustrated and only beginning to make sense of Chimeran. After all you've gone through, you're aware of much more, which means you're ready for more."

"What more do you have to tell me?"

"I'm not going to tell you more; I'm going to show you more. Mirrors come out so the truth can be revealed!"

At his command, the circle of mirrors rose from the ground, surrounding them all.

"Look at yourself. What do you see?"

"Um. . .it looks like me, except. . .in the mirror I'm taller, even though I haven't grown. And there are muscles where I don't have any."

"These mirrors reveal what's inside you—your true self. What you see is your courage. A brave person stands taller and is stronger than one who's afraid."

Another smile broke out on Jacob's face. It felt good to have shown some courage when it was needed.

"Now, take a look at Caldwell—in the mirror."

Since Caldwell had been incredibly brave during the battle, he expected to see a stronger, taller version of him as well. Yet when he looked at Caldwell's reflection, Jacob's mouth hung open. Several times he looked back and forth between the actual Caldwell in the field next to him and the image in the mirrors just to be sure of what he was seeing.

"Is it really you, Del?"

Del shrugged. "Surprise!"

"Why didn't I. . .I should have. . .How could I not see that it was you?"

"You weren't looking for me. And I couldn't say anything," Caldwell apologized, "You never seemed ready to hear it anyway. But didn't it cross your mind that if you lived one life in Chimeran and another in Telluris, other people did too?"

"But I'm still Jacob Tannin in both places. You're like two different people."

"I told you Chimeran was a place where you can be more than you are in your other life," the Man in the Middle explained. "I'm more than Dr. Malson here and Del is more than a smelly kid on the bus. Here, as Caldwell, he could show what a brave warrior he is."

Jacob stared into Caldwell's eyes to see if he could find Del in there without the help of the mirrors. In seconds, he wrapped his arms around him. "Tommy's gonna go nuts."

"Let me get this straight," Andrea said. "You knew him in your other life and you're just figuring out who he is?"

"He was my friend and then I lost him," Jacob answered. "But I really didn't." Then he laughed as he remembered the clue the Great Pine had given him. "Every day and every night they're in your life." Caldwell and Del were in his life day and night; he just hadn't seen it.

"Man, Caldwell Rones and Del Seliger—the same person! What do I call you? Del or Caldwell or something else?"

"Doesn't matter. Either way, it's me, your friend."

"I wasn't much of a friend all the times you

were getting picked on in Telluris. I. . .I'm sorry."

"'Keep your head up, no matter what,' remember? You weren't a brave warrior yet. Besides, those were my battles, not yours. And didn't you save me from the Haggeldies after they captured me?"

"I felt really bad when. . .you know, you died. It was the worst thing ever."

The Man in the Middle put his arm around him. "It felt like the worst thing ever, didn't it? It wasn't. The worst thing ever would be to believe the lies of the Haggeldies. Then you'd have no hope at all. In Chimeran, there's plenty of hope. Here the people you've lost in Telluris are alive. This is the 'something more' I couldn't tell you."

Jacob dropped to the ground. What he'd heard was too wonderful. Far into the night, the two friends sat underneath the Great Pine with Andrea, laughing and sharing stories. As usual, Del did most of the talking while Jacob asked most of the questions—and it felt right.

They finally gave in to being tired and laid their heads against the tree's trunk. Jacob woke up in his own bed with a smile on his face and a question on his mind. "What will Olivia say to me this morning?"

With that, he grabbed another shirt off the banister and made his way down the stairs.

*****

About the Author

Kent grew up on a farm near Oshkosh, Wisconsin where he dreamt about becoming a major league pitcher. When he wasn't throwing a baseball against the barn wall, he was reading every book on baseball in the Oshkosh Public Library. That dream didn't come true – but the dream of marrying someone he loved did. At a dance at Wartburg College in Waverly, Iowa he tapped a beautiful girl on the shoulder and asked her to dance. They've been together ever since. Their family includes four sons, three daughter in laws, and seven grandchildren (all of whom are perfect in every way). After a career as a Lutheran Pastor, Kent is now focused on his passion for writing. Since he never got beyond being twelve years old (at least on the inside), he writes for children. They are the coolest group in the world, after all.

www.KentRaddatz.com
*****

*If you would be so kind,
please leave a review.
Thank you.*

Made in the USA
Monee, IL
04 July 2020